Murder With a Bite of Biscotti

An Ivy Clark Mystery

Kristy T Dixon

To my brothers.
David, Steven, Jared, Sam, Michael, and Aaron.
I know you aren't reading this, but I love you anyway.

Chapter 1

I stood back and looked at the campaign sign. The only way to make it appear straight was to tilt my head. It would have to be crooked because I still had an enormous pile of signs to put up, and time was running short.

Boyd rolled down the window of my gray Kia Soul. "It's crooked."

"My arms are getting tired." I looked at the sign. It wasn't that bad. It said *Vote Boyd Webster for Mayor*. I grabbed one of Jett's signs and put it next to Boyd's. Jett was the only candidate for sheriff, but he'd decided to put signs up just in case that changed. Deputy Ledford had threatened to run but changed his mind when he realized his popularity was low.

Jett and José were putting up signs in one of the other nearby towns. We'd been doing this for days, and I was ready to finish.

"Sorry I'm not more help." Boyd had helped for the first hour, but his shoulder couldn't take it anymore.

"It's fine. I don't mind doing it."

"I thought this would be faster. We should have made fewer signs."

I yawned. "You're running against Mayor Jepson. We need to get your name out. He already has a bunch of followers."

"But do any of them actually like him?"

I shrugged. I'd never heard anyone rave about the current mayor, but he had signs everywhere. It was impossible to move around town without seeing one every few hundred feet. We couldn't put out as many as he did. He had a huge budget and hired help.

Boyd leaned back. "Maybe we should do the rest tomorrow. It's going to be dark soon."

I nodded. "I'm ready to stop."

"Do you think José and Jett did more than we did?"

"I'm sure they did." I wouldn't be shocked if they did twice what we did. They had two people and a lot more muscle behind them.

We drove back into town, and I dropped Boyd off at home, then went to the diner. Carrie had everything under control, so I went upstairs to my apartment. I stepped out of my shoes and greeted my cat. He smelled my shoe, then rubbed around my foot.

"Hey, buddy."

I scooped him up and got him some dinner. While he was busy eating, I went into my room and opened my top drawer. The pile of letters tied together with a blue ribbon jumped out at me. I'd been dying to read these letters, but things kept happening. I loosened the ribbon and picked up the top letter.

I climbed onto my bed and carefully took out the paper. I'd found these letters in Barbra's attic, and being the curious person I am, I'd wanted to read them. Barbra wasn't interested in them, so she let me take them. They had been in the house when Barbra moved in forty years ago, but she'd never cared to clean out her attic.

I looked at the small cursive writing and read—

Dearest M,

I hope this letter isn't too forward. You said your family wouldn't approve of you talking to an almost stranger, but you've been on my mind since I met you while walking down the lane. You deserve better than a no-good drifter. I want to call myself an explorer or adventurer, but I know that's romanticizing it. I have skills but want to see the country before I spend the rest of my life slaving away to survive. Will you meet me near the diner tomorrow at noon? I'll buy you lunch. There is a tree near your house with a large crevice near the bottom. It's the elm near the road and your drive. If you could put your answer there, I'll get it.

Hopefully yours,

R

I wondered who M and R were. If the people had been alive when Boyd was, he might have known who they were. He'd lived in Muddy Creek his entire seventy years. I hoped whoever they were, they had fallen in love and lived happily ever after.

Something fell and broke in the other room, so I put the letter down and went to see what Creepers was up to. I went to the kitchen. The vase from my kitchen table lay broken on the floor, and Creepers gazed at me, daring me to react.

"Were you on the table?" I asked.

He just stared.

I picked up the big pieces and swept the rest. I never see Creepers on the table, but I've suspected he gets up there when I'm not looking.

"You interrupted my letter reading," I told him.

Creepers meowed and batted at my jeans. I dumped the glass in the garbage and put the broom in the closet. I pushed a strand of blond hair behind my ear and peered down at the furry gray monster. He meowed again, so I picked him up and cuddled him against me.

"Are you bored? Did you miss Boyd today?" Boyd usually came over and played with Creepers, but since he decided to run for mayor, he'd been busy and missed a few days. Creepers acted out more on those days.

Someone knocked on the door. I looked at the clock and frowned. It wasn't terribly late, but it was dark outside. I went to the living room and peeked out the window. It was Jett. I opened the door, and he came in.

His brown hair was messy, and he hadn't shaved in a couple of days. He wore a tan shirt with a star and his name. Since the elections were coming up, Jett had been taking more time to present himself neatly lately, so I'd missed this look.

"Did you finish?" he asked. "We didn't."

"No. I'll do more tomorrow. Boyd couldn't do a lot."

"Thanks for helping."

"Sure."

"Why are you grinning like that?"

I hadn't realized I was. "No reason."

He tilted his head. "You look like you're up to something."

I put Creepers on the floor, and he attacked Jett's shoelace. "I'm not up to anything."

He raised his eyebrows.

I put my arms around his neck and ran my fingers through his hair. "I've missed the disheveled look."

He grinned and put his arms around me. "It's been a long few days. Who would have thought putting up signs would take so much time?"

I kissed his jaw, then snuggled against him. "We should have put José and Boyd together so I could spend more time with you."

He ran his hand over my back and kissed my head. "I think it's better this way. We won't get as much done if I'm with you."

I pulled back and looked at him. "Sure, we will."

He grinned and arched his eyebrow. "Now say it with a straight face."

I smiled. "You think you distract me so much that I can't work when you're around?"

"Don't I? Because you distract me plenty." He leaned down and pressed his warm lips to mine. There was no way I could work with Jett and not be distracted, but we still might go faster. José and Jett were quick, and Boyd felt like he was only around for comic relief. I appreciated that, but it didn't get the job done.

"Don't mind me," Boyd said, walking in the front door.

I pulled back and frowned. "Didn't I just take you home?"

"I rode my bike over."

"Why?"

"I haven't seen Creepers all day. He's probably feeling neglected." Right on cue, Creepers came into the kitchen and began purring up against Boyd's legs. Boyd scooped him up and carried him to the couch. "Go back to what you were doing."

"Thanks, Boyd," Jett said. "You have horrible timing."

Boyd chuckled. "I pride myself on it."

"I started reading the letters from Barbra's attic," I said, changing the subject. "Well, I read one."

"Oh?" Jett asked. "Anything interesting?"

"It sounds like a drifter was sending the letters to a girl who lived at Barbra's house. Since I've only read one, I'm not sure where it's going. They would hide letters in a tree near the property."

"Did you find the tree?"

My eyes lit up. "I didn't think to look."

"Do you want to go now?"

I looked at the window. "It's getting late."

"But it might be interesting. What if they left something behind?"

"It would be hard to find in the dark."

"But we could check."

I studied him. "I didn't think you would be interested in this."

He shrugged.

Boyd laughed. "He just wants to get away from me so you can finish your make-out session."

My face grew warm, and I glared at him. "That's not true."

Jett grinned. "It might be."

I bumped him with my shoulder and ignored Boyd's laughter.

"Did you hear Barbra is putting her farm up for sale?" I asked.

Boyd groaned. "Yes. Mayor Jepson is trying to get the city to zone it for development. The city planning committee is discussing it."

"What does he want to develop?"

"Houses. He wants to put in an entire neighborhood. Muddy Creek isn't ready for it, especially with all the condos going in. He's trying to get it all passed before the elections."

"Wouldn't that give Barbra more money from the land?" Jett asked.

"Yes, but it's not a good idea. We don't need the population going up too fast."

"How do you know all this?"

"I'm running for mayor. I need to know these things."

Boyd didn't want to run for mayor, but a bunch of people convinced him he would do better than Mayor Jepson, and he knew they were right.

"What does the planning committee think?" Jett asked.

"They're split. Two members are really against it. One is in favor of it, and the other four are neutral at the moment. There was a big fight between the mayor and the two against it."

"Who's against it?" Jett asked.

"Kara Wilson and Spencer Cunningham."

Jett sat on the couch and rubbed his chin. "Hmm. I don't know Spencer well, but Kara isn't one to back down."

"Nope. Neither is Spencer."

I sat in the recliner and prepared myself for a long, boring conversation I didn't care about.

While Jett and Boyd discussed the situation, I spaced out. I'd planned to spend the evening reading letters, not listening to politics. I was happy to postpone that for Jett, but not for this conversation. After a while, I got up to grab the next few letters and came back out.

I pulled open the first one, unfolded it, and read—

Dearest M,

The memory of your beautiful eyes is what I think of before I fall asleep. Trevor says I'm crazy, and that I'm falling too fast. He's against anything happening between us because he wants to move on. I'll stay here until you're tired of me. I've never been so happy as I've been the past three weeks in your company. You are the dream I never knew I had. I wish it didn't have to be in secret. I still feel your tender lips against mine as I fall asleep. I hope you think of me and have beautiful dreams.

Love,

R

"What's with the grin?" Boyd asked. Both Boyd and Jett were staring at me, and I realized I had a sappy grin on my face.

"Ivy's reading someone's old love letters," Jett told him. "I think we've bored her."

"I wish I knew who these people were," I said.

"Are they the letters from Barbra's attic?" Boyd asked.

"Yes. Did you know the people who lived there before she did?"

Boyd scratched his bald head. "It's hard to remember. The Mortensens lived there for a long time. They had a hard time selling, so they rented the place out for about ten years. There were a bunch of people in and out."

My mouth turned down. "That could make it difficult. Unless the M in the letters is for Mortenson."

"Could be."

I put the letter back. "I wish I had the letters from the other person as well. All I have is a one-sided story."

"Do you know what I wish?" Jett asked. "That someone would take away Boyd's key."

Chapter 2

Two days later, I stood in the diner kitchen and tapped the biscotti I'd made against the island. It was rock solid. I sighed and tossed it into the trash can.

"Don't give up," José said. "Biscotti can be tricky if you don't cook it just right."

"That's my fourth time failing at it."

"You overcooked it."

"I'm going to figure it out." I dumped the rest into the garbage and wiped my hands on a towel.

Anton turned from the salad he was tossing. "Is biscotti even good? I think it looks dry, but it smells good."

I shrugged. "That might just be mine. I've never had it. I just heard someone talking about it and thought I would try."

"People usually dip it in something like tea. That makes it softer," José said.

My eyes lit up. "I should try it with hot chocolate. It's not cocoa season yet, though."

"Where did you get the recipe?" José asked.

"A website called sugarspunrun.com."

"Oh! I use that website sometimes. The woman who owns it has some great recipes. A lot of times, she includes videos on how to make the stuff."

"I saw one, but I didn't watch it."

"Watch it."

"I don't have time to watch videos."

He shook his head. "You don't have time to watch a two-minute video, but you have time to make it wrong four times? You'll save time and ingredients by listening to someone who knows what they're doing."

José was right. I'd watch the video before I tried it again.

Livy rushed into the kitchen, her red ponytail bouncing. "There's a pretty heated argument going on in the party room."

"I'll take care of it," I said. The mayor had a bunch of people in there, and if politics was the subject of the get-together, it might turn sour fast. I walked into the room and stood in the back.

Mayor Jepson stood at the front of a long table. Six people sat on each side. The mayor's face was red, and he glared at a man who appeared to be in his sixties. The man's salt and pepper hair was neatly combed into place and parted on the side. He glared back at the mayor and adjusted his glasses.

The mayor rubbed his double chin. "Listen, Spencer. Muddy Creek can't stay the same forever. I understand your concerns, but you're trying to stop progression."

Spencer stood and pointed at the mayor. "You're only trying to get in with the developers. You don't want what's best for the town. If you did, you would know that a development of that size will strain the town's resources."

"I agree with Spencer," a woman in a blue pantsuit said. She pushed back a strand of brown hair that had come loose from her braid. "We have one gas pump at the hardware store. Only one. It's not even a gas station. We can't support a school. Even if they build, who will want to come?"

"Thanks, Kara," Mayor Jepson said. "You bring up something else. If we develop the land, a gas station is willing to consider coming here. With the condos and a new neighborhood, we might be able to support one. Growth is good. Don't you think people would like it if their kids could go to school here instead of riding a bus for thirty minutes?"

"There aren't enough kids here to make that an issue," Kara said.

"But there could be if we develop."

Spencer's eyes narrowed. "So we're going to create a problem so we can solve it?"

"That isn't the biggest issue here," a woman in her mid-twenties said.

Mayor Jepson's eyes shot daggers at her.

"I'm still not sure why you were invited, Miss Newly. You don't live in Muddy Creek and should have no say in anything."

Miss Newley cocked her head. "The environment should be a concern to everyone, not just people local to an area. Do you know how many animals you would displace on a one-hundred-and-seventy-acre plot of land?"

"It's a farm. It's been used to grow crops, not house wild animals."

She raked her fingers through her windblown sandy curls. "Animals are there just the same."

"Rodents, perhaps."

"And deer, bobcats, and coyotes. There are also hawks and owls."

"And snakes," a short man at the mayor's side added.

The mayor's eyes narrowed as he looked at the man. "I didn't ask for your opinion, Ned."

"Yes, sir."

"When you build, you displace these animals," Miss Newley pointed out.

"One hundred and seventy acres isn't a lot," the mayor argued. "They will hardly notice. They can move over slightly. I don't see the problem."

"But where does it stop? More and more neighborhoods will appear."

"And once again, I wonder how it's your concern." The mayor's eyes fell on me, and he stood taller. "Why are you lingering, Miss Clark?"

"Sorry," I said. "I heard things were getting heated in here, and I didn't want there to be a problem." I didn't know what else to say, but from the frown on the mayor's face, that was the wrong thing.

"I assumed you were here to give your unsolicited opinion."

"Nope."

"Surprising. You're always butting into things that don't concern you. What is your opinion on the matter?"

I shrugged. "I don't know a lot about it, so I can't say."

"Hmm."

"I'll leave if I'm not needed," I said.

"None of these people are needed," he muttered. "This meeting is over."

"We didn't decide on anything," Spencer said.

"I'm still lobbying for the area to be developed. I think most of you agree with me."

I slipped out of the room and back to the kitchen.

"Mayor Jepson likes me less than Deputy Ledford does." I grabbed a rag and got it wet to clean up my biscotti mess.

José looked up from where he was rolling out biscuits. "He doesn't like most people."

"He said I'm always butting into things that don't concern me. I know it's true, but I've helped the city a lot."

"You have. More than he has."

Carrie came in the back door and washed her hands. "Sorry my break went over. I got stuck in line at the grocery store." She put a hairnet over her brown hair and grabbed an apron.

José smiled at her. "No problem. I've always got you covered."

Anton scoffed. "That's not what you say when I'm late."

José whipped a dishrag at him, purposely missing. "That's because you're late about once a week. Carrie's hardly ever late."

"But you wouldn't give her the look I get if she was."

José arched his brow but went back to stirring. "You better believe I'll never give you the same looks I give Carrie."

Carrie turned slightly pink and grabbed a note left on the serving window by one of the servers.

I kept my smile to myself. José and Carrie had started dating, and I was thrilled. I'd hoped it would happen for a while, and it finally did. I took credit for it. They might not have gotten together if I hadn't prodded where it was needed. They had never said they were a couple, but I was pretty sure they were.

"I saw Macey Newley getting into a car when I drove up," Carrie said, grabbing a bowl.

"Who?" José asked.

"She's that environmental activist always tying herself to things in Wichita."

"She was in the meeting with the mayor," I said. "She doesn't want him to develop Barbra's land."

"I bet. I've seen her on TV more than once."

"Do you think the mayor will get his way?"

José nodded. "Probably. There's a lot of money in housing. They could stick over a hundred houses in that area. Lots more if it's high-density housing."

"Who would move here, though?" Anton asked. "It's not like we have a bunch of jobs or anything to draw people. They would have to commute."

"Maybe retired people?" I guessed.

"But the condos are supposed to bring in retired people. How many retired people want to move to a small town called Muddy Creek? People retire to Florida, not Kansas."

"There must be some interest, or I doubt the condo people would be building."

Carrie nodded. "The condos aren't even close to finished, and I heard they've already sold a third of them."

I raised my eyebrows. "Really? I wonder who's buying them."

José looked over his shoulder. "A lot of the older people in town. They're selling their land so they can be close to everything."

"And no one wants to develop their farms?"

"I don't know. I doubt it. There can't be a ton of demand. Barbra's farm is ideal because it's out of town but not far."

"Who's buying their farms?"

"Mostly people who have adjoining farms."

"I should buy a condo," Anton said. "My grandparents left me an inheritance for a down payment on something."

"I bought one," José said. "It should be done in five months."

"Bought what?" Jett asked, coming in from the dining area.

"A condo."

"So no chance of you becoming roommates with me and Boyd?"

José chuckled. "No. I found a different roommate."

Carrie spun around and held up her hand. A diamond ring glittered on her finger.

"What?" I exclaimed, jumping to my feet. I hurried over, and Carrie showed me the ring. I hugged her.

"Wow, you two move fast," Jett said. "When's the wedding?"

José shrugged. "Yesterday."

"What?" I echoed.

"We went to Wichita and eloped."

"Are you serious?" I asked. Carrie didn't seem like the one to tease, but José would.

"Yep," Carrie said. "We're too old to mess around."

"You aren't old," José said.

She smiled.

"I can't believe you're here," I said. "You should go somewhere fun. We can manage."

José raised his eyebrow. "Oh yeah?" José and Carrie were the only two full-time cooks.

I smiled. "I didn't say it would be easy. Why didn't you tell us?"

"We decided yesterday. We didn't want to waste time, and neither of us wanted a big wedding."

"I didn't even know you were officially dating," Anton said, putting a plate out the serving window.

"People these days date for a long time, waiting to make sure everything is perfect or that they've found the right person," José said. "If it takes years to know, then how can it be right? I love Carrie, and I want to spend my life with her. Why wait years just to say we did?"

Carrie beamed, and Jett gazed at me with a look I couldn't interpret.

"You two need to get out of here," I said. "You don't get married one day and come back to work the next. We'll be fine. I'll call Tiffany and see if she can come in, and Anton can get more hours."

"Yippee for me," Anton said, but he was smiling. "Seriously, go. We can manage. I've been thinking about asking to go back to full-time anyway. My online classes aren't taking up as much time as I thought they would."

José looked doubtful, but Carrie grabbed his hand and pulled him out the door.

"They didn't take off their hairnets and aprons," I said. "They are so adorable."

"But what were they doing?" Anton asked, looking at the food José had halfway prepared. I pointed at the sticky note José was using to fulfill an order. "You finish what you were doing, and I'll do this."

Jett shook his head. "I never saw that coming. José doesn't strike me as the impulsive type."

I smiled and stirred. "I love it. José's right. If they know they want to be together, why wait?"

Chapter 3

"I'm thinking of selling the house as is." Barbra raked her hand through her purple hair. "If a developer gets it, they're just going to bulldoze the place anyway."

We stood in Barbra's attic, and I frowned as my eyes scanned all the wooden boxes. "You can't do that until I've been through everything in the attic. I'll move fast."

"It will take a while to get things moving. The mayor wants to rezone the land, but Spencer Cunningham wants to buy it. Who knows what will happen?"

"Spencer Cunningham? Isn't he the man on the city planning commission?"

"Yes."

"Why would he want to buy it?"

"I have no idea. It's a nice spot of land."

"He's against it being developed."

"If he wants to buy it, that's not a surprise. Have you read all the letters yet?"

I shook my head and opened a box. "I haven't had time. I've read five or six. I'm dying to know who sent them and what the story was. There are still quite a few letters left, so they might shed some light on it. I hope the two people fell in love and ended up happy."

The box had some dingy-looking tablecloths inside. Those could be tossed.

"I love that you care about this stuff," Barbra said, looking around the dusty attic. "I just see junk when I'm up here, and you see treasure."

"I can't believe you didn't want to read the letters."

"Maybe when you're done."

"Did you hear about José and Carrie?"

"Yep. I'm happy for them. I know Carrie's been lonely living by herself. I never saw it coming. He's got to be a good eight to ten years older than she is."

"Once you get to a certain age, does it really matter?"

"I suppose it doesn't. I think they'll be a great couple."

"I'm going to open all the boxes and see what's inside. It goes against what I want to do, but if I spend a day looking in every box, I'll never get finished. That's why it takes me so long to read the letters. I read one, then I stare at it for too long."

"I bet you do. I'm going downstairs. Call me if you need anything."

"Thanks." I opened as many boxes as I could, then I went through inspecting everything. Most of it was disappointing. People must have shoved stuff up here because they didn't know what to do with it. I'd found the letters the first day, and they ended up being the best thing up here. There were things Barbra could sell, but nothing as exciting as the letters.

I got home in time to go for my nightly walk with Jett. When he wasn't on duty at night, we would walk around the town square. We didn't get a lot of time together, so Jett suggested taking the walks so we could see each other at least once a day.

I ran a brush through my hair and talked to Creepers while I got ready. I knew it was silly to get ready to go for a walk in the dark, but I did it anyway. I brushed my teeth and rushed out to meet him.

Jett stood in front of the diner, looking up at the sky. He held Conan's leash, and the little white dog wagged his tail when he saw me. Jett turned and smiled. I linked my arm with his, and we began walking.

"Any place you want to walk past tonight?" he asked.

"No."

"Did you go to Barbra's today?"

"Yes. I looked through all the boxes but didn't find anything worth mentioning. I was hoping for some old photographs or something."

"Photographs of M and S?"

"M and R."

"Right."

"I was hopeful. If the house was rented out for ten years, and a lot of people lived there, it might be impossible to figure out who they were."

"I'm sure you will. This is the type of mystery solving I can get behind. The people are probably all dead, and you won't be stumbling onto something dangerous. How was the diner today?"

"Crazy. I need to take better cooking lessons from José. I made the worst spaghetti. I told José he couldn't come back for three days, and now I regret it. Why is regular food so much harder than baking? I need to hire more people so everyone isn't working so much, but no one is looking for a job like that."

"When the condos get put in, it might be easier to get people. Especially since some of them are going to be geared toward families. There might be more teenagers looking for part-time work."

"Probably, but I can't hire teenagers as cooks, only as servers. Well, I guess I could, but they would have to be mature and willing to learn."

"If it's easier to get servers, you could make Livy a cook. You already know she works hard."

"True, but then she might get too distracted by working close with Anton."

"Does she still want to go to cosmetology school?"

I shrugged. "She hasn't mentioned it. Anton's going back to full-time. If I could get one more full-time cook, we could stagger it so people only worked normal shifts. José works too many hours, and now that he's married, he'll start resenting it."

"I thought Carrie's sister wanted more hours?"

"She said that a while ago but keeps saying she isn't ready yet."

We walked past the construction site for the condos. We passed it most nights. It was interesting to see the progress. So far, there were only basements, and a few of them had frames. We didn't pause long because Conan wanted to move fast.

Jett's phone buzzed, and he pulled it out. "Ledford needs me to sign something."

"At this time?"

"Yeah. He forgot to have me do it, and it needs to be sent tonight. I'll walk you home first." We picked up the pace and made it back in good time.

I went up to my apartment and got ready for bed. I curled up on my bed with the bundle of letters and Creepers at my side. I read through a bunch of them, but none gave me any clue as to who these people might be. I opened the third-to-last letter and read:

Dearest M,

Your cousin almost caught me delivering the last letter. I ended up hiding in the tree, waiting for him to leave. It's getting harder to deliver them when people are watching. Now that your family suspects something, I worry. I won't be able to meet you tomorrow. Trevor will drop off a letter next time to avoid suspicion. He said it's the last time he's helping me. He wants to leave Muddy Creek, and he's threatening to go without me. Take care, and I'll talk to you soon.

Love,

R

I opened the next letter.

Dearest M,

You have to let me talk to you. I need to explain. I know you're angry, but everything you've been told by your family is a lie. Trevor is going to deliver this letter, then he's leaving. He wants me to go with him, but I don't want to leave even though you hate me now. My heart is broken when I think of you out there believing those things about me. Please meet me once more. I know you said you won't, but please.

The letter wasn't signed. I frowned and looked at the last letter. It was the only letter with an R on the envelope, not an M. It had never been opened. I stared at it for a moment.

I wanted to open it, but I felt guilty. This letter must have been written by M and never delivered.

I carefully slid my finger under the seal and took out a piece of paper. The handwriting inside was different from the other letters. My heart sped up as I read:

Dearest R,

I will never send this letter because I killed you.

"What?" I muttered, putting a hand to my heart. I kept reading.

I knew better than to let my family influence me. I did it anyway, and this is the result. How will I ever live with myself? You were everything to me, and I threw that away. I loved you so much. Why didn't I listen? Why did I act in haste? I can't go back and rewrite the past. What's done is done, and now I must move forward alone.

M

I read the letter over and over again. What happened? I got up and put the letters away, then climbed back into bed and stared at my dark wall. I wasn't sure how long I stayed that way, wondering what could have made M do something like that.

The following morning, I slept in. I had a terrible time falling asleep, and I woke up disoriented. I took a quick shower and headed down to the kitchen. I worked quietly until José and Carrie came in.

"I know you told us to stay away for three days, but we know you need us," José said.

I laughed. "We need to hire more cooks."

"I was in here by myself all morning," Anton said. "I should get a raise."

"Sorry," I said. "I couldn't sleep last night."

"Why not?" Carrie asked as she put on her apron.

"You know the letters I've been reading?"

She nodded.

"The last one was the woman confessing to killing the man she was in love with."

"What? That's crazy."

"And now I need to figure out who they were. Before, it was only out of curiosity, but now, I feel like it's important."

"Did you look online for anything about a murder?"

"Not yet. I was going to ask Boyd if he remembered anything like that happening. I could ask Jett to look back in the police records."

José grabbed a pan. "Go now. We've got this."

I ran up to my room and grabbed the last letter. Jett's location was programmed into my phone. I looked at the screen and saw he was at the sheriff's office, so I hurried over and barged in the front door.

"Hi, Ivy," Jane greeted me. She sat at the front desk in front of a computer.

"Good morning. Is Sheriff Malone in?"

She pointed at Jett's office. I knocked on his door, then peeked in.

"Hey," he said from his desk. "Is something wrong? You look distressed."

I went in and sat in the chair in front of his desk. "I finished reading all the letters."

"Did you find out who they were?"

"No. This is the last one." I handed it to him, and he read it. His forehead creased. "Man. That went in a different direction than you thought it would. And I know you. You aren't going to sleep until you figure this out."

"Do records go back that far? Can you find anything on a murder?"

"I'm not sure. We don't even know when it happened, so that makes it hard. Barbra's house is old."

"Will you try?"

"Sure."

"This is going to drive me crazy. It seems like it would have caused a stir in Muddy Creek."

"Unless no one knew about it. No one would go looking for a drifter."

"I'm going to go talk to Boyd. If it came out, he would know."

I left the sheriff's office and walked across the town square. When I got to the condo site, the woman from the mayor's meeting had chained herself to the fence outside, and a man wearing a hard hat was talking to her. Macey. That was her name.

"Please, leave," the man was saying.

"Not until the mayor agrees to leave the land alone. First, these condos go up, then the mayor's little neighborhood. The next thing you know, this place will be huge, and all the wildlife will be gone."

She made eye contact with me and called out, "Come join me! A lot of voices make a difference."

I walked over. "Places change. It's part of life."

She frowned. "So you want your little town to become another Wichita? The small-town values will all be lost."

"I like the town the way it is, but these condos will help a lot of the older people in the area come together."

"I don't care about these condos. I don't want the other land getting developed."

"So why bother these construction workers?"

"There's nowhere to chain myself over there, and I want to keep it that way. Save the trees!" she called out. "No, no, I won't go until you plant some trees!"

I wandered away. I thought she was lobbying for the animals. Farmland didn't have a lot of trees. I made it to Jett and Boyd's place and knocked. Conan barked, and the door opened.

"Hi, Ivy," Boyd greeted me.

"Can I come in?"

"Of course."

I entered and went into the living room and sat on Jett's old blue sofa. I handed Boyd the letter, and he read it.

"Wow."

"Do you remember any drifters coming through in your time?"

"Not really, but that isn't something I would have paid attention to."

"Do you remember a murder?"

"Nope."

I sighed. "I need to figure this out, but I don't know where to start."

"Have you talked to Brian? Librarians are all about research, right?"

I tapped my lip. "That's a good idea."

A pounding on the door made us pause. Boyd hobbled to the door, and I followed.

"You're limping."

"Remember when I tore up my knee? I think I overdid things yesterday, and now it's hurting."

He pulled open the door, and Barbra stood there.

She smiled. "Hi, Boyd. Do you know where Ivy is? She's not answering my texts."

"I'm here," I said, waving over Boyd's head.

"Oh, good."

I looked at my phone. "You only texted me ten minutes ago."

"Yeah, I went to the diner and texted you when you weren't there, then I came here. I figured Boyd would know."

"What do you need?"

"I wonder if you could come over and look at my land. Someone's been digging in a few spots, and it's making me nervous."

I frowned. "Digging? With a shovel?"

"I don't think so. My guess is they're using some kind of machinery. My question is why? Nothing good ever comes from people being where they aren't supposed to be."

Chapter 4

"My bet is someone used a mini excavator," Boyd said as we stood looking at the holes surrounding a large elm tree. There weren't many trees on the farm, but elm trees were scattered around. Barbra said they had left the trees for shade when working the fields. They could sit under them and eat lunch without returning to the house.

"What's a mini excavator?" I asked.

"It's something you can sit in and drive. It has a hydraulic arm and bucket that can scoop dirt quickly. It's a lot faster than using a shovel to dig a hole. A lot more fun, too."

"Are those the type of tracks it would leave?" I pointed at eight-inch tread marks all over the area.

"Yep. It rolls along like a tank."

Barbra studied the tracks and pointed. "The tracks go past my house and over to the road. Wouldn't I hear something like that go by?"

"They have some electric excavators that are fairly quiet. I have one out in my garage at my old house. I locked everything in there and told the renters not to touch it."

"Do you think someone might have stolen it?" I asked.

Boyd chuckled. "No. In a place like Muddy Creek, I bet most of the farmers have one."

"I might even have one," Barbra said. "Of course it would be old and possibly falling apart. I haven't been in the barn in years."

"Why dig here?" I wondered, walking around the holes. "What would someone gain by it?"

Barbra shrugged. "Nothing I can think of. I should have sold all this land years ago. It's just sitting here neglected. I sold a bunch of land when my husband died, but I should have gotten rid of all of it."

"Why didn't you?"

"Sentimental reasons, I guess. I also hoped one of my kids might want to farm it someday, but none of them are interested in farming."

"Is this the only spot disturbed?"

"I don't know. I could see this from the window, so I came out to look."

I couldn't see anything but the tracks and holes. I was a little confused as to why Barbra got me instead of Jett.

"Should we fill the holes in?" Boyd asked. "I might not be able to for a few days with my sore knee."

"I can't imagine what someone was trying to do here," I said, "but you should tell Jett so he can have a record of it. I wonder if it might be the builders who want to develop the land. Maybe they wanted to see what the soil was like."

Barbra nodded. "That makes total sense. They should have come to me and told me so I wouldn't be paranoid."

"It might be something else. I'm only guessing."

"I'll talk to Jett, and he can decide whether we fill it back in."

I took Barbra and Boyd back to town and dropped Barbra off at Jett's office and Boyd off at the diner. He wanted to spend time with Creepers. I parked and walked to the library. Brian was inside showing a teenager how to scan a book.

"Hey, Brian," I said. "You aren't hiring help, are you?"

He laughed and ran a hand over his curly black hair. "I know, I know. I said I never would, but I am."

I looked around the empty library. "And it's a good thing."

He tilted his head and gave me a big smile. "Tease me all you like. I'm making some changes. Gena, will you go put the books on the rolling shelf away?"

Gena smiled, showing her braces. "Yep. Thanks for hiring me, Mr. Hooper. My mom has been bugging me forever about getting a job." She grabbed the rolling cart and walked out of sight.

"I'm cutting back library hours," Brian said. "I've had long hours since I opened and finally realized I'm wasting my time. All I do is sit here reading and making displays. It was fun for a while, but I'm getting bored. I've realized I'm boring because it took me a long time to get tired of it."

"What will you change the hours to?"

It wasn't odd for businesses in Muddy Creek to have shorter hours than I was used to. The small grocery store was only open for seven hours a day, and the hardware store even less.

"Three hours a day and closed on Saturdays and Sundays."

"That sounds about right for Muddy Creek. What will you do with all your time?"

"I decided I should probably do something that makes money. I have more money than I could ever spend, but it's starting to feel like I'm not contributing to anything."

"Any ideas of what you might do?"

Brian's eyes lit up. "Not exactly, but I have a short-term job lined up that I'm excited for."

I leaned against the tall desk and rested my arms on it. "Oh?"

"A man called me the other day. He said his sister is starting a library in a place a few hours from here. She doesn't know what to do or how to run one. It will be like this one. A privately owned library. He's going to pay me to go help her get started."

I grinned. "If you smile any harder, your face might crack."

"I'm so excited. The most fulfilling thing I've ever done was start this library. The best part was the beginning. Getting it all set up and figured out. The man bought a building that needs a bit of repair work. I can help with a lot of that. It's been gutted, so we can plan it out and make it perfect."

"You sound like the right man for that job."

"If it works out, I might try to get other jobs like that. It wouldn't have to be libraries. I'm sure I could do other things. You didn't come here to hear this. What can I help you with?"

"I love hearing about it. I did come for a reason, though. I've been going through Barbra's attic."

"That's a big undertaking, from what I hear."

"Yeah. And I found some old letters."

Brian's eyes went wide. "That's like finding gold."

"That's what I thought. They were from a drifter who came through Muddy Creek and fell in love with someone who lived in Barbra's house before she did."

"I love this already."

"It didn't end happily. The girl wrote the last letter. She admitted to killing him."

"Dang. And I know you. You're trying to figure out what happened."

"Yes. Can you help me figure out who they were?"

He pulled out a pad of paper and a pen. "What do you know?"

"Her name started with an M and his had an R."

"So we don't even know the name?"

"No."

"About how many years ago?"

"No idea. There are no postmarks, and the letters aren't dated. It was at least forty years ago because it was before Barbra was there. All I know is the letters of the names, that he was a drifter, and he had a friend named Trevor who traveled with him. Oh, and the person with the M had a cousin."

Brian tapped the pen against his lip. "This isn't a lot to go by. I can figure out all the people who lived in the house. That shouldn't be too hard. A drifter might be harder to figure out. He could be from anywhere."

"But if he was killed, there should be some record."

"Unless she hid the body. Who would look for a drifter? They would figure he moved on."

"That's what Jett said." My forehead creased, and I tapped my fingers against the desk.

"Don't look discouraged. I bet we can easily figure out who the woman was. Give me a day and come back tomorrow. I'll have a list of everyone who lived there."

"Thanks, Brian. You're the best."

"Text me anything helpful you might think of."

I nodded and told him goodbye. When I got to the diner, Boyd was outside talking to Mayor Jepson. His hands were on his hips, and he didn't look happy.

Mayor Jepson was pointing his finger at Boyd and appeared to be giving him a lecture. "You aren't qualified to be mayor. You should step down and save yourself the embarrassment."

Boyd's eyes squinted. "What makes you more qualified? Because you've done it before? Don't forget, we both grew up here on farms. That means we're on equal footing."

"You're too undisciplined. I doubt you can follow any rules."

"You follow rules? That's a laugh. You only got the job because no one ran against you last time."

I could see patrons of my diner looking at the two of them out the window.

"Let's go inside, Boyd," I said, taking his arm.

"Do you hear this guy?" Boyd huffed. "He has no right to lecture someone on following rules."

"Drop out," Mayor Jepson said. I noticed a big purple bruise on the mayor's forehead. "All you're doing is embarrassing yourself and wasting time. You'll never win."

"If you believe that, why are you trying to get me to drop out? Wouldn't you rather win by running against someone? You want me to quit so you can get voted in without any effort. You have low popularity."

"Watch what you say, or you'll regret it."

The short man from the mayor's meeting came rushing over. "Mayor, we need to be leaving." I wasn't sure whether he was as small as he appeared or if the mayor was just a big man in comparison.

"Hush, Ned. No one wants your advice."

Ned gulped and nodded.

I pulled harder on Boyd's arm and dragged him into the diner.

"He's trying to get to you," I said. "Don't let him."

"I know," he muttered. "That man drives me crazy."

The people at the tables all gave Boyd curious stares.

"Sit, and I'll have Livy bring you some food."

He nodded and went to an empty table.

I went into the kitchen and grabbed a mixing bowl. I was going to learn to make biscotti. This time, it would work.

"Boyd just had a fight with the mayor," I told José. "I think he needs some comfort food."

José shook his head. "I'm on it. Boyd needs to be careful. He doesn't want to stoop to Jepson's level."

I placed some butter in my bowl and got out the sugar.

"Trying biscotti again?"

"Yes."

"Biscotti means twice baked in Italian."

"I baked it twice last time."

"After you bake it once, it needs to be completely cool before you cut it and bake it again. Did you do that?"

"No. That would take too long."

"That might be why it isn't working."

I sighed. "I hate being patient."

José grinned. "I know."

"Okay. This time, I'm following all the instructions." I grabbed the hand mixer and creamed the butter and sugar. "It says to add the eggs one at a time. Does that really matter?"

"I don't know, but do you want to risk it?"

"I guess not."

Carrie looked up from her brownies. "Adding the eggs one at a time makes it easier to mix, and it will turn out smoother and more consistent."

José walked over and kissed Carrie's cheek as he went to the fridge. "Isn't she brilliant?"

I smiled as Carrie blushed.

"I think so," I said, adding vanilla to my mixture.

"Did you watch the video this time?"

"No."

"Watch the video. It might save you from making mistakes."

The bell tinkled, and I glanced up to see Jett enter the diner. He came into the kitchen and looked over my shoulder. "Cookies?"

"Biscotti."

"I'm guessing that's a food."

I smiled. "The few times I've made it, it's been more like a rock."

He sat on a stool at the island. "I've looked into the past cases in Muddy Creek. I can't find anything about a murdered drifter."

"Any unsolved murders? Or mysterious people who were killed here?"

"Nope."

"So M got away with murder." I grabbed another bowl for my dry ingredients.

"It looks that way."

"I have Brian on it. I'm sure he'll figure something out. He said he can figure out who lived in the house. Then I can narrow it down to people who start with an M."

He grabbed a handful of chocolate chips. "I'm going to Barbra's to look at the holes dug in her land. Any ideas about that?"

"No. I can't think of any reason for a person to do that."

"Well, I'm off then."

"Are you keeping Kara locked up?" José asked.

I glanced up. "Kara Wilson? The woman on the planning committee?"

Jett nodded. "She threw eggs at Mayor Jepson. Forty years old and she's solving her anger like a thirteen-year-old. She hit him right in the forehead. He looks like a toddler who is just learning to walk. I gave her a lecture and let her go."

José shook his head. "Kara's always had a temper. She chased down the postal worker once because he forgot to stop at her house. She lectured him, and I never saw the man again. Either he got a new route or she made him quit."

"She opposed the mayor on everything. Lots of people backed down when they dealt with him, but not Kara."

"I can't help feeling bad for Ned," I said. "I don't know who he is, but the mayor is always being mean to him."

"Ned Forshaw is the mayor's assistant. He must get paid well because Jepson is always barking at him, and Ned keeps working for him." Jett stood and pointed into my bowl. "I'm off to Barbra's. Good luck with... that. Save me a piece if it's good."

"I will. And it's going to be. This time, I'm following the directions."

Chapter 5

Creepers crawled across my face, waking me up better than any alarm clock. I sat up and rubbed my eyes. "It's too early." He didn't care. He took over my vacated pillow and stretched out.

I got up and figured I should take a shower. Or maybe I should go running. I hate running. I told José I gave up on it. He tried to get me going, but it was rough. One of the biggest reasons was because of the early morning runs. Since I was up anyway, I should probably give it a second chance. I pulled on my black leggings and a white T-shirt.

José wouldn't be out for another fifteen minutes, so I had time to meet him in front of his house. I sped walked through town and over to his place. With luck, he would be there. I didn't know where Carrie and José had decided to live.

A few minutes after I arrived, José came out in his shorts and T-shirt. He peered through the darkness at me.

"Ivy?"

"It's me."

"What's wrong?"

"Nothing. I got up early and thought I should go for a run."

"Great."

He was lying. I was interrupting his running time. I could see it from the fake smile.

"You don't have to stay with me. I just thought we could start together for the first minute."

He laughed. "First minute?"

"That's about as long as I can run."

"Okay. I usually walk for a few minutes before I run."

We walked across the square. The sun hadn't begun rising yet, and the only sounds were the crickets and an occasional owl.

"What made you want to run again?" he asked.

"Creepers crawling on my face."

"That would do it."

We walked past the construction site. A chain-link fence completely blocked off the area, making it so we would have to walk around.

"Did you hear something?" José asked.

I stopped and listened. "No."

"It must be me."

A loud crack sounded, and a man yelled out, followed by a crash. José took off at a run, and I followed. We went around the tall fence until we came to the gated entrance. It was hard to make out what was what in the dark. I could see some of the tall scaffolding, but not well. José lost me, and I scanned the area. I detected movement to the right; it sounded like someone scaling a chain-link fence. I ran that way, but no one was there.

I turned on my phone's flashlight and looked around, trying to see anything out of the ordinary or José. Something on the ground caught my eye. It appeared to be a debit or credit card. I bent over and picked it up. A noise made me jump.

José was running toward me. He had his phone to his ear. "It's Mayor Jepson," he said. "He must have fallen from the scaffolding."

"Is he hurt?"

"He's dead."

I blinked and waited while José finished the 911 call. He put his phone away and took a deep breath.

"Are you sure he's dead?" I asked.

"Positive."

"Why was he up there? And in the dark?"

"Who knows?"

"Can you show me where it happened?"

José shook his head. "You don't want to see."

I nodded. I trusted José.

We went over by the gate and waited until we saw police lights coming near. Jett's truck stopped, and he got out. His eyes fell on me, and he frowned.

"What are you doing here?"

"I was out running with José."

He nodded. "Where's Jepson?"

"I'll take you," José said. I followed them at a distance.

Jett squatted down, I assumed to make sure he was dead. "Did you see anything?"

"No," José answered. "We heard the fall and ran over."

"I heard someone climbing the fence. At least I think that's what I heard." I held up the card I found. "They might have dropped this."

Jett took the card and shined a flashlight on it. He frowned and looked at me. "It's Boyd's debit card."

My eyes went wide. "Boyd can't be involved."

"My guess is the fall was an accident. Jepson probably climbed up the scaffolding and fell."

"There was a cracking sound first."

"It must have broken."

José's eyes narrowed. "But if Ivy heard someone climbing the fence, that means someone else was here. The mayor might have been up to something."

I chewed on my lip. "This is going to look bad for Boyd. He couldn't have climbed the fence. Not with his knee. He wouldn't have any reason to be here or to talk to Jepson."

"The card could have been there for a while," José said. "Boyd could have lost it before they even started construction here."

"True," Jett said. "He's lost his wallet more than once this last year."

"Now what?" I asked.

"We wait for the paramedics. At least I do. The two of you can go if you've told me everything."

"I'm not leaving you here alone," I said. "I'll wait with you."

"I'm going to finish my run," José said. "I have my phone if you need me."

"Stay in one place," Jett told me. "Don't touch anything. I'm going to look around. I called Ledford, so he should be here any minute."

I nodded and folded my arms. The cool air reminded me that summer was coming to an end. Fall was my favorite season, but I wasn't ready for another Kansas winter. I didn't stay where I was, but I didn't touch anything.

More police lights flashed across the square. That must be Ledford. I sat on an overturned bucket and waited. The ambulance came, and after a while, I wondered if Jett had forgotten I was there. I should be getting ready for the day. The sun had come up, and the birds sang in the trees. I stood and yawned.

Ledford came over to me. "How do you do it?"

"What?"

He rubbed his mustache. "Always end up in the middle of everything."

"Talent, I guess."

He frowned.

"This time, I was minding my own business. It just happened. Where's Jett?"

"Sheriff Malone saw some suspicious people hiding in the shadows. He chased them, and I haven't seen him since."

My heart sped up. I knew Jett was the sheriff, and it was his job to do these things, but that didn't mean I didn't panic when he might be in danger. I looked frantically around.

"Don't panic," he said. "They were big, burly guys. I'm sure they weren't fast. He probably caught them and took them to the office."

"Big, burly guys? Why didn't you go with him?" I demanded.

Ledford shrugged. "He told me to stay here."

"Which way did he go?" If Jett was hurt, Ledford better watch out.

"Hey, Ivs?" Jett said from behind me. I spun around. He looked fine. "Are you alright?"

I rushed at him and jumped into his arms, smashing my lips against his. He stumbled back slightly but didn't drop me. He placed me on my feet, and I kept my mouth sealed to his. My heart hammered against my chest. I heard Ledford chuckle behind me, but I ignored him.

Jett pulled away and looked down at me. "What's going on?"

I hugged him. "You scared me! Why would you go chasing two people by yourself?"

"What are you talking about? I wasn't chasing anyone."

"But Ledford said—" I turned and glared at Ledford. "You lied?"

Ledford grinned. "Calm down. It was just a joke."

My eyes shot daggers at him. "I didn't think you knew how to tease."

He shrugged. "It comes over me every once in a while."

"Not nice, Ledford," Jett said.

"Can you really complain? No woman ever kissed me like that. You should be thanking me."

Jett turned to me and grinned. "He has a point."

My eyes narrowed. "You better watch out, Ledford."

I took a step toward him, but Jett intercepted me. He bent over and put me over his shoulder. "Come on. I'll take you home." He began to walk toward the diner.

I used my hands to push myself up so I could see Ledford and his silly smirk. "Mark my words, Ledford. You're going down."

"Oh, yeah?" Ledford asked. "What are you going to do?"

I smiled. "I'm going to find you a woman who will kiss you just like I kissed Jett."

Jett chuckled. "Is that a threat? It doesn't sound like a threat."

"Well, his face went pale. You can put me down."

"And you won't attack Ledford?"

I rolled my eyes. "When have I ever attacked someone who was just standing there?"

He put me on my feet and took my hand.

"I can walk back by myself if you need to stay here."

"I have everything blocked off, and the paramedics took the body. Ledford can keep things under control for a minute."

"Did you go to Barbra's yesterday?" I asked.

"Yeah. There are tons of holes, but only around the trees."

"Not just around the one tree?"

"Nope. They're around a bunch of elm trees. I'm not sure why only elms. It looks like it's happened over a while. Some spots are more freshly dug up than others."

"Weird." We got to the diner and walked around back. "Is there a reason someone would dig around trees?"

"Not that I can think of."

My mouth turned down. "I have so many things going through my head. It's hard to keep them straight. And now I'll have to find a woman I dislike enough to get her to kiss Ledford."

Jett laughed softly. "That was the most pathetic threat I've ever heard."

"I know. I'm tired. I'll see you at lunch. You're off at noon, right?"

"Yep."

I started up the steps, but Jett grabbed my arm. I turned. "Yes?"

Jett's eyes twinkled. "Just out of curiosity, do I have to be in danger to get another kiss like that?"

I wrapped my arms around his shoulders. The step I was on made us the same height. I kissed him lightly, and his arms encircled my waist. "I would kiss you like that forever if you wanted me to."

The humor left his face, and his eyes pierced mine. "Marry me."

My eyes went wide, and I sucked in a breath.

"I planned to be down on one knee saying something poetic, but I don't feel like letting you go. I love you, Ivy. More than anything in this world. You've made me a better person, and I want to spend my life with you. Will you marry me?"

My eyes searched his, and I smiled. "Yes. I love you." I felt tears well up in my eyes. I ignored them and leaned in for a kiss. His warm lips caressed mine, and all the things I'd been worrying about escaped from my thoughts.

I pulled away and pressed my forehead to his. "Shouldn't you be at a crime scene?"

"Probably. It's not going anywhere."

He kissed me again, then stepped back and pulled a small box from his pocket.

He opened it and took out a diamond ring. The center stone shimmered in the dim light, square and brilliant, flanked by two smaller stones on either side. It wasn't flashy, but it was elegant—classic, with a touch of old-fashioned charm. He slipped it onto my finger. It fit perfectly.

"I love it."

"I love you."

Chapter 6

I spent the morning pacing my apartment. Jett needed to get back to the crime scene, and we hadn't discussed how we would tell people about our engagement. I didn't want to go down to the kitchen because someone would notice the ring. We should probably tell our parents first. My parents were in Arizona, so it would have to be a phone call.

At noon, there was a knock on my door. I opened it to see Jett.

"Is everything okay?" he asked. He looked nervous. "José said you haven't been down today."

I wrapped my arms around him. "I know it's silly, but I feel like I can't go down because everyone will see the ring, and we need to tell our parents."

"You could take it off."

I frowned. "I don't want to."

He kissed my nose. "Then let's tell them."

"My dad's a bit old-fashioned. He might be a little annoyed that you didn't talk to him first."

"I did talk to him."

"You did? When?"

"The last time he was here."

"That was a long time ago."

"I figured I might not see him for a while. We'd already told them it was in our plans. I pulled him aside later, and he told me whenever we were ready, we had his blessing."

"Should I call them?"

"No. Come down to the diner. My parents are there. So are Boyd and Barbra. I told them to come for lunch. Let me see your phone."

I handed it to him, and we walked down the stairs into the diner. My stomach was tied in knots. Jett's parents, Carol and Tanner, were there, and Opal, Barbra, and Boyd were at another table. Ledford sat by himself eating a fry.

Jett was dialing something on my phone. He put it on a video call. My mom's face popped onto the screen.

"Sheriff Malone, is that you?" my mom asked.

"Yep. Is your husband nearby?"

The screen showed my mom moving around the room. My dad popped up next to her. Everyone in the diner was looking at Jett since he was talking at normal volume.

"What's going on, Jett?" my dad asked.

Jett turned the phone so my parents could see the people in the diner. "The diner is pretty packed. Hey in the kitchen!" he called. José, Carrie, and Anton all came out. "Ivy and I just want you all to be the first ones to know that we're getting married."

The room was silent for a moment, and then cheering erupted. Carol Malone rushed over and gave me a hug. Jett was saying something to my parents, but I couldn't hear him over everyone else talking.

"I can't believe he didn't warn me!" Carol said, wiping at her eyes. "I hoped it would happen."

The next thirty minutes were a blur. Everything settled down, and I escaped to the kitchen.

"Congratulations," Carrie said. "You look overwhelmed."

"Maybe a little," I said, taking a piece of the biscotti I'd made yesterday. It had finally turned out decent. Watching the video and obeying the rules made the difference. I put it on the island and grabbed a mug. I hadn't eaten today.

"When did this all happen?"

"This morning." I grabbed a packet of hot chocolate and poured it into the mug, then filled it with hot water.

"It's about time," José said. "Jett's been carrying that ring around since February."

My eyes went wide. "Really?"

"He said he had to wait for a moment when it came out naturally. He was worried about looking like an idiot."

"He never looks like an idiot," I said, stirring my hot chocolate. I sat on a stool and dipped the biscotti into the mug, then took a bite. I thought it might taste funny with the chocolate chips, but it was perfect.

"They do say love is blind," Anton teased.

"I believe it," José said. "I still can't believe Livy puts up with you."

Anton laughed. "Neither can I."

Boyd burst into the kitchen. "Did you hear the mayor died?" Jett was right on his heels.

We all went quiet. I could tell from Anton's and Carrie's faces that they already knew. I wondered if Boyd knew about his card.

"What I wonder," he said, "is why the mayor was up there in the dark? It seems suspicious to me."

"What I'm wondering," Anton said, "is where Boyd's going to live when Ivy and Jett get married."

"I don't know, but I'm way more excited to go home every night to Ivy than to Boyd." Jett grabbed a piece of biscotti and shoved it in his mouth.

Boyd chuckled. "I'll probably go back to my house. Although I've been thinking I might buy one of the condos. It's nice being in town and not being out away from everything."

"Are you going to live in Ivy's apartment?" José asked.

"We haven't talked about that yet," I said. "I suppose Boyd could live in my spare room."

Jett frowned.

"Nah," Boyd said. "They need that room for Conan and Creepers."

"I need to go to the library," I said, not ready to make all these decisions. "Brian was helping me with some information about the letters."

"I'll go with you." Jett took my hand, and we walked to the library. When we arrived, Brian was sitting at his desk, looking bored. Brian loved the library, and he always looked enthused. He must really need a change.

"Hello," Brian said, his signature smile springing up. "I was hoping you would come."

He grabbed a paper and put it on the desk. "Here's a list of the people who have lived in Barbra's house. None of them started with an M, so I looked into the census."

My eyes scanned the paper. "Did you find anything?"

He put another paper down. "Before Barbra moved in, the Cunningham family rented the house for about a year." The paper in front of him had columns and lists. He pointed at the paper. "See here, it says *Head of house Maxwell Cunningham*. Then the people listed under his name are those who lived in his house and how they're related. You have Patty Cunningham–wife, Spencer Cunningham–son, George Hammer–boarder, and Mandy Cunningham–niece."

My eyes went wide. "Mandy starts with an M. In the letters, there's something about her cousin. She must have lived with her uncle."

"And Spencer Cunningham is still around," Jett said.

"The guy on the city planning committee?" I asked.

"Yes. He would have to know what happened to her since she's his cousin."

My eyes lit up. "And if he's alive, that means she might be as well. How old do you think he is?"

Jett shrugged. "Sixty-five?"

"She could be around the same age." I clasped my hands. "This is the most exciting thing! I might figure this out."

Jett tilted his head and gave me a half smile. "The most exciting thing?"

I smiled. "The most exciting thing besides the fact that I'm going to marry the most wonderful man in the world."

"Nope. It's too late. I'm wounded."

Brian smiled, but coming from Brian, it wasn't a very happy smile. "You two are engaged?"

I showed him my ring.

"Congratulations."

"Thanks. I wonder if Spencer would talk to me about it. Did you find anything about a drifter?"

"No. I tried looking up a drifter named Trevor, but I didn't get anything. And no strange unsolved murders from Muddy Creek."

"Hmm. At least I have a name."

Jett nodded. "But remember, it might not be the right person."

"I know, but I bet it is. Should we go talk to Spencer? Do you know where he lives?"

"We can if you want. He lives outside town, but not far."

"Then let's go. Thanks, Brian."

He nodded. "Anytime."

"Can we walk?" I asked as we exited the library.

"It would take forever. Let's take my truck." We began our walk back to the diner. "Did Brian seem a little... different?"

I nodded. "He's getting tired of the library."

"He spends way too much time there. You would think that would be a place to talk to a lot of people, but not here."

"He's going to limit the hours and hire someone to work there. Then he's going to help someone start a library in another city. I bet that helps."

"Did you see his eyes die when he found out we were engaged?"

I narrowed my eyes. "No. I don't see why he would care."

Jett put his arm around me. "Brian has a crush on you."

I laughed. "He does not."

"Denial."

"Brian has never even hinted at liking me."

"He drops anything to help you."

"Because he's nice."

"And he likes you. You don't see it because you aren't looking for it. I see it all the time. It drives me crazy, but you're right. Brian's nice, and he will keep it to himself."

I frowned and watched the dirt pass by under my feet. Could Jett be right? I would never want to hurt Brian. I shook my head. I would have noticed. Brian was fifteen years older than me.

"I think you're wrong."

"He buys things for your cat."

"So do you."

"Yeah, because I love you."

"He loves Creepers."

"I understand you cat people love all cats. Brian has a ton of cats. He can spoil his own cats. He was flirting with you through your cat."

I laughed. "You're so weird."

"I know, but I'm right."

We got to the diner and climbed into Jett's truck, then drove out of town. I didn't want to think about Brian and anything Jett said about him, so I focused on the case.

"Shouldn't you be at the construction site?" I asked.

"I think we have what we need. The mayor went up on the scaffolding, and it broke. It was an accident."

"But so many people hate him. Are you sure?"

"No, but that's what it looks like."

"What about the person I heard climbing the fence?"

"You might have been hearing things because you were scared."

"I wasn't that scared."

"I'll look into it some more. I have forensics there looking for prints, just in case."

"I can't believe everything that's happened today. My brain is on overload."

Jett grinned. "I can't believe you invited Boyd to live with us in your little apartment."

"I love Boyd. He's like my grandpa."

"I love Boyd too, but I've lived with him long enough to know we don't want him there all the time."

"I hope he gets a condo. He could be neighbors with Barbra and José."

"He probably will. Did you take his key?"

"No. If I do, he won't be able to play with Creepers."

"But if you don't, he'll pop in all the time."

Chapter 7

Spencer Cunningham led us to a sitting room in his large farmhouse and gestured for us to sit on the sofa. He sat on a wooden rocking chair. His eyes hadn't left Jett since we knocked on the door. He rubbed his brown and white goatee.

"Is there a problem, Sheriff?"

"No problem. We just have a few questions. Well, Ivy has some questions."

Spencer tilted his head. "Go ahead and ask."

"Is it true you once lived in Barbra Todd's house?"

His eyes narrowed. "Barbra? I'm not sure I know her."

"She's about seventy-five and usually has purple hair."

He smiled. "Ah. I have seen her around. I'm not sure what house you're referring to. My family rented out a farmhouse while we built a house for a short time."

"It's the land the mayor wants to develop."

"Oh. Yes. I did live there. I'm actually hoping to buy that land if they don't develop it. It's a nice piece of land."

"We saw your family's name on the census."

He leaned back and crossed his legs. "Why were you looking us up on the census?"

"I was helping Barbra clean out her attic, and I found some letters. I believe they were written to your cousin Mandy."

A shadow crossed his face. "I forgot she stayed with us for the summer. Mandy was always quiet and did her own thing. She was easy to forget."

"Is she still alive? I'd like to give her the letters back." It was mostly a lie. I wanted to confront her about killing R.

He shrugged. "I'm not sure."

"You don't know if your cousin is alive?"

He leaned forward and rested his arms on his knees. "The summer Mandy stayed with us was the last time I saw her. She spent most of the summer reading, then she started sneaking out. I was a few years older and thought I was too old to worry about a younger cousin. My parents wanted me to figure out what she was doing, but I didn't try hard."

"The letters are from a man. They're love letters."

"That's interesting. I wouldn't have believed she would talk to someone she didn't know. She was shy. I'm not sure what happened. She came home one night upset. My mom talked to her. The next day, she was gone, and I never heard anything about her again."

"Did you ever try to contact her?"

"No. Our parents weren't close. I can't remember why she came. I think her parents were on a long holiday, and she didn't want to go or something like that."

"Do you know how I could get ahold of her, or anyone who might know where she is?"

"Sorry. No."

"You didn't know anything about the man who sent her letters?"

"Nothing. I'm sure my parents did. I know they were upset about something regarding her. They're dead now, so I'm afraid I can't be of any help. You might as well burn the letters. I doubt she would want them now."

"Could she have run off with the man?"

"Possibly."

"Did you hear about anyone disappearing around that time?"

He sat up straight. "Disappearing? No. Who?"

"I don't know. I just wondered if anyone might have been looking for your cousin." I knew I wasn't making a lot of sense. We should probably go before he gets suspicious.

"It's pathetic of me, I know, but I haven't even thought about Mandy in years. I'm sorry I can't help you."

"It's fine. Thanks for talking to us."

"You work at the diner, right?" he asked. "You were there the other day when Mayor Jepson was making a fool of himself."

"Yes."

Spencer turned to Jett. "Do you have any sway with the mayor? Maybe you can get him to see what developing that land would do to Muddy Creek."

I looked at Jett, and his mouth turned down. "Mayor Jepson died this morning."

Spencer's eyes went wide. "What happened?"

"He fell from some scaffolding at the condo construction site."

"Wow. That's too bad. I mean, I don't know if anyone actually likes the man, but that's not a great way to go."

"People dislike him?" I asked, trying to get any information I could.

"Everyone I know. Even his wife can't stand him."

"Do you know her?"

"Not well, but from what I hear, she won't even appear in public with him anymore."

"We should go," Jett said, standing. "Thanks for your help."

Spencer nodded. We went to Jett's truck and got in.

Jett started the engine. "He's not exaggerating. When I went to talk to his wife to let her know what happened, she rolled her eyes and said it figured. She didn't look upset at all."

"When did you talk to her?"

"When you were waiting at the construction site."

"I must have been there a lot longer than I thought."

"The mayor lives behind the square on the opposite side of the diner. It only took a few minutes." He looked at me as we drove into town. "I'm starting to feel bad. The mayor dies, and right after, I propose. I'm sorry. I should have waited. That wasn't sensitive of me, but it just felt right."

I rubbed his arm. "It was perfect. Your job isn't full of a lot of light-hearted moments. You have to put those aside and live your life, and I'm sure it's hard. You can't miss your own happy moments because of it."

His brow softened. "You're good for me. I've wanted to propose for a while but didn't want people to think I was rushing things. When José and Carrie got married, I realized I didn't have to care what others think is best, only what we do."

"I'm glad you didn't wait."

I stood next to Boyd on Barbra's land and studied the dirt that had been dug up around a tree. Conan ran around barking and chasing bugs.

"I can't see any reason for anyone to do this," I said. "What could the point be?"

"Maybe someone got some new equipment and wanted to test it out," Boyd said.

"But why test it on Barbra's land, and why only around elm trees?"

"Shade?"

"They're doing it at night."

"It could be someone from a surrounding farm. They might not realize where the boundaries are."

"The first hole we saw was obviously on Barbra's land. It wasn't that far from the house."

"People get crazy when it comes to property lines."

"Who owns the land around Barbra's?"

"I'm not sure how far hers goes. Kara Wilson and her husband own the land behind hers. She's on the planning committee."

"The one who threw the egg at the mayor."

Boyd chuckled. "That's her. Kara's always been a spit-fire."

My phone rang, and I pulled it out. Jett's name shone up at me. "Hello?"

"Guess what?"

"What?"

"The scaffolding Mayor Jepson was standing on was tampered with. When I examined it closer, I noticed some cuts in the wood. The boards broke but only partway. The rest looks neatly sawed through."

"I'm not surprised."

Jett chuckled. "I didn't think you would be. That's not all. The metal sides were missing some of their screws. I've searched all around and can't find them, so I'm betting someone took them."

"Do you want me to come?"

"No, I just wanted to let you know so you don't have to go snooping."

"How will knowing stop me? Now I have more reason to look into it."

Jett sighed. "I should have known you would say that. I'm going to get to the bottom of it before you can get yourself in danger. Don't you have something else to do, like find out where Mandy Cunningham went?"

"I did some searches last night. Mandy Cunningham is a popular name. There are tons I need to eliminate."

"Good. You work on that."

I smiled. "I will."

I hung up and watched Boyd pull Conan out of a hole.

Boyd set him on the ground. "Stay out of there. Now look. You're all covered in dirt."

Conan barked happily and bounded after a butterfly.

Boyd dusted off his pants. "We should have brought Creepers. He needs more outside time."

"He doesn't appreciate it."

"But he's getting better."

"I think he's getting fat. He probably does need more exercise." I climbed into the three-foot hole and ran my hand through the loose soil. I didn't know what I expected to find, but there had to be a reason for all of it.

"Teenagers could be doing it as a prank," Boyd said. "I can imagine me and my buddies doing something like that in high school."

"Should we put up cameras? Even if we put them near Barbra's driveway, we might see something."

"That sounds complicated, and we don't know if they'll come back."

"We could dig around the trees and see if we find any-thing."

"And those teenagers will be laughing their heads off at us. We've seen holes near seven trees. Digging would be a slow, painful process."

"How many oak trees are on the land? We could look around the ones that haven't been dug around."

"Jett said there were only three more that hadn't been disturbed yet."

"We could dig near those."

Boyd let out a long sigh.

"You don't have to help."

"It's not that I don't like to dig for hours and hours for no reason. It's just that I'm getting old. My body can't take it."

"That's fine." I didn't need Boyd to hurt himself. "I'll take you back to the diner, and you and Conan can play with Creepers."

"Do you even have a shovel?"

"No, but I bet Barbra does. Didn't you say you might have a mini excavator?"

"I might, but I haven't kept up on the maintenance for any of my machinery. Besides, you don't know what you're doing, and it takes time to learn how to use those kinds of things."

"I could ask around town and pay someone to dig it up."

"But then you're advertising to whoever did it that you're up to something."

Boyd was right. I didn't want to alert the person, or people, and risk not figuring out what they were doing.

"Don't you have enough to do with figuring out the letters?"

"Yes, but this is happening now. Whatever happened with the letters was a long time ago. This might be connected to the mayor's murder."

"We're calling it a murder now?"

"Oh, I didn't tell you. Jett said the scaffolding was tampered with."

"So you're connecting that to holes in the field?"

"Well, those angriest with the mayor at the moment are mad because of this land. We know a bunch of people don't want the land developed, and at least one person wants to buy it."

"I hear multiple people want it. The farm is a mess now, but it used to be a profitable piece of land."

Conan jumped into the hole and moved around my feet. I climbed out and looked across the land. I'd never lived on a farm, so I didn't know what made one spot better than another. Conan jumped out and ran over to a deeper hole on the other side.

"Don't fall in," I said, right as Conan slipped into the hole. We rushed over. Conan yapped happily and moved the dirt around with his nose.

"Crazy dog," Boyd said. "Get up here."

Conan tried to jump out of the hole, but he was too short. "What do you have there?" I asked. I slid down and picked him up. I grabbed something dirty and hard and pulled it from his mouth. I turned it in my hands and frowned. It was slightly porous and brown. I pushed the dirt off, and a chill went up my spine. Something protruding from it resembled a tooth.

I handed it up to Boyd and wiped my hand on my pant leg. "What does that look like to you?"

Boyd studied it. His brows came together, and he glanced at me. "It looks like a jawbone."

Chapter 8

I stood near Deputy Ledford's desk in the sheriff's office as he finished a phone call. I'd tried to call Jett, but he must be too busy with his crime scene. Ledford hung up and looked up at me.

"Miss Clark?"

"I found this on Barbra's property." I handed him the supposed bone. "Actually, Jett's dog found it."

Ledford studied the bone, and his eyes narrowed. "This looks like a human jawbone."

"That's what Boyd said."

"It's old."

"I think I might know who it belongs to," I said. "Well, not who, but I might know who killed them and buried them there."

He peered at me. "Let's hear it."

"I found some old letters in Barbra's attic."

"Right. Jett told me about that. So you think the person in the letters killed this person and buried them there?"

"Yes."

"It makes sense to me."

I raised my eyebrow. Ledford agreed with me and didn't talk down to me. That was new.

"Someone's been digging around Barbra's property. I bet someone knows the body is there and is trying to find it. The mayor wanting to develop the land might have sent someone into a panic."

Ledford rubbed his chin. "They must not know where it was buried except it was near an elm tree. Sheriff Malone said the only areas disturbed were near elm trees."

"Whoever was digging must have just barely missed the body."

"The entire body is there?"

"I'm not sure. I didn't see anything else. I'm guessing. I freaked out when I saw this."

Ledford jumped up. "Well, let's go. Do you have any tools there?"

"No. Should we get some?"

"No. We just need to see if there's anything else down there. If we find something, we need to call forensics. They can come take care of it and do it carefully." Ledford grabbed his keys, and we rushed past Jane.

"Jane, when Sheriff Malone comes in, tell him I went off with Miss Clark. We're going to Barbra Todd's farm."

We went to Ledford's car, and I got in. I never would have thought I would be driving to a potential crime scene in Ledford's car.

"Tell me what the letters said? The sheriff told me some, but I wasn't paying close attention."

I explained it all on the way, and Ledford was caught up when we got to Barbra's. I led him to the tree and the hole.

"So it was this one?"

I nodded.

Ledford climbed carefully into the hole and looked up. "Where was he when he pulled up the bone?"

"Just to the right of your boot."

He put on a pair of gloves, then bent down and moved his hand through the dirt. He pulled something from the dirt and immediately put it down. "I probably shouldn't have done that."

"What is it?"

"The rest of the skull. I need to talk to the sheriff, and we need to get some people here to take care of it."

"What's that?" I asked, pointing near the place Ledford had been searching. Something shiny caught my eye.

Ledford squatted back down and pried something from the dirt. "It's a pocket watch." He brushed off the dirt and turned it in his hands. "This should point to someone."

"It had to be Mandy."

"It's a men's watch. It might belong to the victim." He unclasped it and looked inside. "It has some numbers inscribed." The biggest smile I'd ever seen on Ledford overtook his face. "It's the coordinates to somewhere."

"Are you sure?"

"Yep. I'm boring. I study strange things, and I geocache."

I wrinkled my nose. "You look for rocks?"

He rolled his eyes. "No. Not geodes. You don't geocache? You're the type of person geocaching is made for. People hide small containers all over the place and leave a clue. Inside is a list, so when you find it, you write your name on the list and hide it again."

"Hmm. That does sound like something I'd do."

My phone rang, and I grabbed it. "It's Jett. Hello?"

"Hi, Ivs. Jane just told me you ran off with Ledford? That's a bit of a shock the day after our engagement."

"Ha ha. We're at Barbra's near one of the holes. We found a body."

"Of course you did. Anyone you know?"

"No, it's old. I think it's the person Mandy Cunningham killed."

Ledford leaned in near my phone. "Sheriff, we need forensics to dig it up. We only have the skull."

"I'll send them," Jett said. "I can't come. Stay with the body until they arrive. We should probably assume the person digging around there doesn't want it found."

"Alright."

"Love you."

"I love you. Bye." I hung up and stuffed my phone in my pocket. "He said we should stay here until forensics gets here."

Ledford nodded. "It might take a while. They have to come in from Wichita."

I nodded and sat in the dirt. Spending time with Ledford was not on my list of things I wanted to do. Thinking of things to talk about for more than a few minutes would be worse.

"The coordinates on the watch shouldn't be too far. I wonder where it goes." He pulled out his phone and snapped a picture of the inscription on the watch, then put the watch in a baggie he pulled from his pocket.

"Do you think the fingerprints survived?"

"No, but it's possible." He put something into his phone. "The coordinates are down near the creek. About three miles from here."

"And I bet you aren't going to tell me where?" I guessed.

Ledford's lips puckered, and he scratched his cheek thoughtfully. "If the forensic people come fast enough, I'm thinking of letting you tag along."

I blinked. "Really?"

"Better than having you search by yourself. With my luck, you would find it first, even without the coordinates."

I grinned. "That's unlikely. The creek goes on for a long time."

We sat for what felt like hours, but in reality, it was only one. Jett called to tell me the forensics van was in Barbra's driveway. I ran over and led them to the hole, and Ledford explained everything to them. One of the other deputies from town was with them. Ledford put him in charge, and we left to follow the clue on the watch.

Ledford drove down a dirt road I'd never been on before. He pulled over to the side of the road and turned to me.

"We'll have to walk from here."

I hurried out, and we tramped through the weeds, away from the road. The sound of the creek reached my ears, and I sped up.

"The water must be higher than last year," I said. "It was like a drizzle when I saw it last."

"We had heavy snow last winter. I bet it rose a lot."

It felt strange having a normal conversation with Ledford. I tried to remember his first name. Not that I would ever dare to call him by it. He'd made it clear early on that he appreciated people calling him by his full title.

The creek came into view. It wasn't only a little bigger than last year. It had risen significantly. The bank was raised on the sides of the creek, and the water looked like it was two feet deep and five feet wide. Not huge, but huge compared to what it was.

"This is it," Ledford said, looking at his phone.

Birds chirped, and a bee buzzed near my ear. My eyes scanned the area. Wildflowers grew near the water, and tall green grass blanketed the ground. Nothing stood out more than anything else.

Ledford walked around the area, searching the ground. A strange mound of rocks caught my eye. The rocks were all about two feet across and were unnaturally piled on top and around each other.

"What do you think about this?" I asked, pulling one rock off and tossing it to the side.

"Someone definitely piled those like that." He took one off and moved it away. We pulled the rocks away until only one was left. It was bigger than the others. Ledford shoved it to the side, and I looked down into a dark hole. He pulled out a small flashlight.

"Did someone dig this?" I asked.

"It looks like the opening to a cave."

My brows knit together. "A cave? In the ground?" I thought caves were all in the mountains, but then I was from a place with mountains, so that was what I knew.

"It's not uncommon," he said, leaning down to look in. He got on his stomach and stuck his head inside. "It's a good size."

"How deep?" I asked.

"Ten feet. There's an incline, so we could slide down. I have some things in my truck we should take. I'll be right back." He got up and jogged away. I still couldn't believe we were doing this. I mean, I would do this, but it didn't seem typical Ledford.

He came back carrying a rope, lantern, and two head-lamps. He handed one to me, and I put it on.

"Do you think anyone's been down here since the murder?" I asked as I put the light around my head.

"It's hard to say. The watch might belong to the dead guy, or it might belong to the killer. If the killer had something down there, he probably came back for it. If it belonged to the dead guy, I bet no one's been down there since."

"Do we need the rope to get down?"

"I don't think so. We can probably slide. I'm just bringing the rope as a precaution. I'll go first." He put his feet in first and squeezed into the dark abyss. I counted to sixty, then stuck my legs in and began moving in. The light bounced across the walls. Ledford stood at the bottom of the incline. He looked up at me, his headlamp shining in my eyes.

I squinted and made my way slowly down like a slide. The incline was smooth and cool. My feet tried to slip, but I concentrated hard with each movement. When I got to the bottom, I stood and held in a sigh of relief. I didn't want Ledford to know I was nervous.

"Are you good?" he asked.

"Yep." The cave was beautiful. It had shining stalagmites and stalactites. I never would have imagined something like this underground in Kansas. Something white and smooth covered the ground.

The spider silk, woven between stalagmites like tangled curtains, sent shivers down my spine. I scratched my head. Spiderwebs always made me uneasy. Where there were webs, there were spiders, and with the amount of webs I saw, there were probably hundreds.

"It looks like the path goes down this way," Ledford said, walking toward a narrow opening in the walls. I followed and batted at a spiderweb I walked through. He squeezed through the crack, and I went after. He stopped and pulled something from his face and wiped at it.

"What is it?"

"Lots of spiderwebs. No one's been down here in a long time. You're welcome. I'm taking most of them in my face, so you should have a clear path."

I tried to ignore the ones that touched me. "I appreciate it." We were between two smooth walls, and they were close enough together that they were lightly touching both sides of my body. I never thought of myself as claustrophobic, but my heart sped up, and I was breathing funny.

Twenty paces in, we came out into another cavern. It looked similar to the first area, but the ceiling was higher. I could hear running water, but I hadn't seen any so far. Ledford held up the lantern, illuminating the area.

"We aren't under the creek, are we?" I asked.

"Umm... I doubt it. I think we went in the opposite direction. I bet this place gets flooded in wet years.

"I bet our phones don't work down here. We should have told someone where we were going."

"Sheriff Malone wouldn't have let us go if we told him."

I raised my brow. "Now you sound like me. Are you going to get in trouble?"

He shrugged. "My shift ended right before you found me. I was about to go home, but I was intrigued and wanted to check out Barbra's farm and the body."

"And your shift ending means it's okay that we're here?"

"Probably not."

I hugged myself for warmth and wished I had a jacket or at least long sleeves.

"We're just calling this exploring with friends."

I laughed. "We're friends?"

"Okay, exploring with people we've learned to tolerate."

"That sounds more realistic. Look at that." I pointed at an area near the cave wall. It looked like a waterfall that had been frozen in time. "It's so pretty."

He nodded. "I love caves. I used to explore them with my brothers."

I tried to take it all in. My headlamp scanned the area, making light dance across the walls. "I feel like we should see pirate bones holding a treasure chest."

Ledford chuckled. "That would be quite the find in Kansas."

"I guess."

"I think we have to crawl through there."

I looked down at the spot Ledford was pointing at. A small opening, only big enough to squeeze through, met my eyes.

"I'm not sure about that. It's small."

"Is the famous Ivy Clark scared?" Ledford asked, raising his eyebrow.

"No. I just don't think we'll fit." I was terrified. I wasn't sure if my teeth chattering was from the cold or fear.

Ledford got on his hands and knees and looked in. "We can do it. It will be tight. If it gets too bad, we can back out." He crawled in.

I wrinkled my nose and crawled in after him. The air was musty and thick. I hoped it wouldn't trigger my allergies. "How far does it go like this?"

"I can't see the end yet."

All I could see was the backside of Ledford. Not the best view, but I was glad he wasn't behind me. A faint scampering sound behind me made me turn my head. I bumped into the wall and cringed. When I turned back, my cheek scraped against the wall.

"Are there rats in caves?" I asked.

"Probably."

"Can you go faster?"

Ledford picked up speed, and I crawled quickly behind him. My knees were killing me, and my hands didn't feel great either. Ledford stopped.

"What is it?" I whispered.

"We didn't find a pirate, but we might have found a treasure."

Chapter 9

I crawled out of the tunnel and gaped at the cavern in front of me. Treasure was the wrong word, but there was a small area full of... stuff. It was all covered in thick dust. There was fancy silverware, small farm equipment, a box full of liquor, and other odd things.

"I bet whoever put this here stole it," Ledford said. He pulled on his gloves and opened a suitcase. Money wrapped in bands fell to the cave floor. "Dang," he said, stuffing it back in. "Whatever they were up to, it wasn't good. This money came from a bank in Wichita."

"How can you tell?"

"The name of the bank is stamped on the bands. Besides solving a murder, we might have just solved a bank robbery from years ago."

"We haven't actually solved the murder, and we don't know who stole the money."

"No, but finding it will make someone at the bank happy. I'm definitely putting this on my résumé."

Two sleeping bags lay neglected on the ground.

"The man in the letters said he was a drifter, and he was traveling with his friend. I bet they were holed up here and stealing things."

"Probably."

Something was poking out of one of the sleeping bags. I went over and pulled out an envelope. It matched the envelopes the letters from R were in. I opened it and pulled out the paper before Ledford could stop me. He was busy studying the suitcase. Unfamiliar writing met my eye.

Ripley,

I'm done with this place. The law will catch on to me as soon as people notice missing things. Too many people in town have gotten a glimpse of me. We've wasted enough time in this place. Break things off with the girl, and let's move. No girl is worth getting caught for. I'll deliver your letter, then I'm out of here. I'll take the cash and be done with the rest.

Trevor

"Ripley!" I exclaimed. "He's the R!"

"What?" Ledford asked, turning. I handed him the letter, and he scanned it. "Interesting."

"Now what?"

"We take pictures and leave."

"I wonder why Trevor didn't come back for the money."

Ledford gestured to the suitcase. "The dust on the suitcase isn't as thick as the other stuff. I bet Trevor comes back every now and then for more money. It doesn't look like anyone's been here recently, but it hasn't been sitting empty for forty years."

"Should we go get Jett?"

Ledford frowned at me. "He's not going to be happy when he sees you."

"Why?"

"You have blood all over your face. What happened?"

"I scraped the wall." I pulled a tissue from my pocket and wiped at it.

"You're only smearing it. Let's go."

I followed him back through the cave. Going back was easier because I knew what to expect, and there were fewer spiderwebs. When we got to the incline to get out, I glanced up. It appeared steeper going up.

"You go first," Ledford said.

I nodded and began climbing. The cave under my hands was slick. I focused and made it to the top without too much trouble. I pulled myself halfway through the hole and grabbed the ground near the cave's entrance.

"Ivy!" Jett exclaimed. I turned and saw him rushing to me. He bent down and pulled me the rest of the way out and to my feet. "What in the world?" He crushed me in a hug.

"It's a cave."

"Why were you in it? You're bleeding."

"It's fine."

Ledford popped out of the cave, and Jett jumped back in surprise. "Ledford?"

"Hey, Sheriff." He stood and brushed off his pants.

Jett turned to me. "What were you doing? I saw your location on my phone. It came here, then stopped and showed no signal. I've been up here having a heart attack."

"Sorry."

"It was my fault," Ledford said.

Jett cocked his head. "You?"

"Yep. We found a watch near the body. It gave coordinates to this place. We found the cave and went in."

"I expect that from Ivy, but not you."

"Hey!" I protested.

"I know. Sorry," Ledford said.

I handed Jett the letter. "Trevor and Ripley were living down there. Ripley is the R in the mystery. I bet that's an easier name to find than Trevor. There's money down there and a bunch of stuff we figure they stole."

Jett sighed and placed it in his pocket. "We'll block this area off and have a team come through. People who are experienced with these kinds of things."

I nodded. I didn't want to go back down there.

Jett pulled something from my hair and tossed it.

"What was it?"

"Spider."

I shivered.

"Come on. I'll take you home, and you can shower. Are you good, Ledford?"

"Yep."

We walked up to the vehicles, and Ledford drove off. I climbed into Jett's truck and buckled.

Jett started the truck and turned to me. "I think you're a bad influence on Ledford."

I smiled. "I couldn't believe he brought me."

He handed me a wet wipe, and I cleaned the blood from my cheek.

I told him about the things we had found from the time Conan unearthed the jawbone.

"It does seem like whoever dug up Barbra's land probably knew about the body," he said. "I wonder if Mandy came back. I'll check the B&B to see if they have anyone who might be her."

"Someone might have helped her hide the body."

"It's possible. Maybe her aunt and uncle? They're both dead, though. Spencer Cunningham, perhaps? He didn't seem to know anything, but would he admit it? He could have been helping his cousin, then they decided to cut contact so no one would tie it to them." Jett kept muttering guesses to himself.

"I bet it's even tied to Mayor Jepson's murder," I said. "Whoever killed him didn't want the land developed."

"We know Spencer is against it."

"And Kara Wilson. Also, that environmental woman."

We drove up to the diner and got out. Jett walked me up to the door. "I have a few things I need to do, then I'll meet you for dinner."

"Sounds good." I kissed him, then went inside. Boyd was sitting on the couch watching a movie. Conan lay on his lap, and Creepers slept near his head.

"What happened to your face? Did you find the whole body?" he asked.

"I went back with Ledford. We found a skull."

"You look like part of a mountain fell on you."

"We found a cave. I'll tell you about it after I shower."

I went into the bathroom and looked at my face. I'd had worse. If I looked closely enough, I could still see a white line where I'd cut my cheek on the top of a fence.

By the time I showered and changed, I was tired. I yawned and went and sat in my recliner.

"Tell me all about it," Boyd said.

I told him everything that happened from the time I left him in town.

"Man," he said. "I wish I'd seen the cave. I bet Jett has it blocked off."

"I don't think it's somewhere you should go. You might have a hard time getting around."

"Yeah, I don't suggest getting old. If you could barely squeeze through some of the places, I never would have made it," he said, patting his stomach.

I grabbed my laptop from the coffee table and flipped it open. I searched for drifters named Ripley. I didn't really think that would help, but you never know. Once that search failed, I tried searching for missing people named Ripley. Still nothing. I searched for Ripley and Trevor.

"I'm not sure what to search. Ripley doesn't seem like a common name. I might need to talk to Brian. I'm not sure whether he's left town yet."

"You know," Boyd said, "now that I think about it, I do remember something a long time ago about things getting stolen. Everyone in town was getting worked up. I didn't feel like it affected me, so I don't remember the details."

"Hmm. This is going to drive me crazy."

"I thought you would be more concerned with the mayor's death."

"I think it's connected. I believe whoever helped Mandy bury the body killed the mayor so the land wouldn't get developed and the body wouldn't be found."

"Or someone might just hate the mayor."

I looked at Boyd. "Did Jett tell you about the debit card?"

"Yep. I'm not worried. I lost that thing over a month ago. The bank was nice enough to send something to Jett telling him I hadn't used it in that long."

"You didn't get it replaced?"

"Nah. I don't use it that much."

Creepers stood on the couch and yawned.

"Is there a way to see everyone who wants to buy Barbra's land? Spencer Cunningham does. He seems nice enough, but Mandy is his cousin. He might want to buy it so no one will ever figure out what she did."

Boyd frowned. "I doubt we can find out everyone who might want the land. I've heard several people want to make offers. Kara Wilson wants it since it's connected to her place. It would make her farm bigger."

"How long has she lived on her farm?"

"All her life. She grew up there, and her parents gave it to her when she got married. They retired and moved to the city."

"She's too young to have been involved in anything regarding Mandy, but I guess we can't assume the mayor's murder is related to Mandy. It's only a guess. Kara and her husband could want the land bad enough to kill Jepson."

He nodded. "She did pelt him with an egg. That was a big goose egg she gave him. I heard he was going to press charges."

"Would that make her mad enough to kill him?"

"I dunno. Don't rule out Ned Farshaw."

"The mayor's assistant? What would he have to gain?"

"Well, it turns out the mayor decided to fire Ned if he got reelected. He's tired of Ned not being able to read his mind or something. It would have been crazy to fire Ned. No one could find an assistant as organized as he was."

"Really? Did Ned know he was getting fired?"

"Yep. Someone let it slip."

"You sound like you've been gossiping."

Boyd laughed. "It was book club today, and you know how that goes. If something is going on in town, the book club knows about it."

"I need to talk to Ned."

"Don't forget about Jepson's wife. I'm even scared of her."

I nodded. I needed to make a list. There were too many people to keep track of.

Chapter 10

The smell of José's pizza filled the diner. A youth group rented out the party room and had requested it. I'd never tasted it before, but those kids were in for a treat if it was as good as it smelled.

I sprinkled flour on the large island and grabbed my rolling pin. These cinnamon rolls might not be as good as I hoped because I'd let them rise too long. I put the dough on the island and began rolling it out.

José handed a pizza to Livy, and she took it out, then he followed her with another. When he came back, he passed me and said, "Ned Forshaw just came in."

"Did he get a table?" I asked.

"Yes."

I looked at my dough. It was already a mess. "Anton, will you finish my cinnamon rolls?"

"Sure."

"Are you going to talk to Ned?" José asked.

"No. I'm going to his office."

José raised a brow. "Are you sure that's a good idea?"

"No. Do you want to come?"

He laughed. "Carrie, can you take care of things for about thirty minutes?"

"No problem."

I was glad he agreed to come. I didn't know where Ned's office was. When we entered the city building, an older woman sat behind a desk. She was the only person I could see.

"Do you have an appointment?" she asked, looking over her glasses.

I wondered who we would have an appointment with. The mayor was dead, and his assistant was at the diner.

"Is anyone in?" I asked.

"One of the city council members. The clerk might be back there. I can't remember."

"We're going to go back and talk to John," José said.

She nodded and looked at her computer. We passed her desk and walked down a long hallway. The doors all had name plates next to them. When we got to Ned's, we tried the door. It opened right up.

"Who is John?"

"No clue. The secretary is getting forgetful. They need to replace her, but no one wants to upset her."

"There isn't a lock," I observed.

"I bet the mayor didn't want people to lock him out," José said, flipping on the light.

The office was small. Ned must be a neat freak. There wasn't anything on the desk that didn't have to be there. Besides the desk, the only other thing was a filing cabinet. I pulled on my gloves and started searching through the desk drawers. José opened the filing cabinet.

"I've never seen a desk this organized," I said. "It doesn't look like there's anything interesting."

"This doesn't either. Just documents, and there aren't many."

"Let's check out Mayor Jepson's office while we're here."

We left the room and went next door. The mayor's office was significantly larger than Ned's. It wasn't as neat, but it wasn't messy either. I went straight to the mahogany desk, and José opened a closet.

On top of the desk was a tear-off calendar. The page on top was the day after the mayor was killed. Either someone tore it off or the mayor had done it by mistake a day early. I opened the drawers one by one. The bottom drawers had all the torn-off pages from the calendar. The top was from the day before the murder. It contained a list of appointments.

"The calendar page from the day the mayor was killed is missing," I said.

"I bet Jett took it."

"Has he looked in here?"

"I don't know. I would guess so. You know more about what he does than I do."

"He doesn't tell me about cases unless he feels like he has to."

I grabbed a pencil and lightly scribbled over the calendar page.

"What are you doing?"

"Seeing if I can make out what the page from the day before said. It should have lightly imprinted on this page, so scribbling over it should let me see what it says."

"I think that only works on TV."

"Nope. I've experimented before." Small white letters appeared on the paper. I picked the calendar up and squinted at the light letters. "It says meet Ned for picture."

"That's all?"

"Yes."

"That could mean anything. Ned's his assistant, so he probably meets him all the time."

I nodded. "True. I wish it said where he was meeting him."

"Jett's going to be annoyed you scribbled on something that might be evidence."

I looked at the calendar and frowned. "If he already looked, does it matter?"

"I don't know. I bet they don't want people touching anything until this is all solved."

"Do you know where Ned lives?"

"Yes."

"Let's go there."

"We don't know how long he'll stay at the diner."

I took a deep breath. "Call Carrie and ask her to give him a free dessert. A big one."

José grinned. "Have you seen Ned? I doubt he can eat a meal and a dessert. But I'll call her."

By the time we reached Ned's house, I was about to change my mind. Ned didn't have a lot of motive to kill Jepson. Jepson was a jerk to him, and maybe wasn't going to rehire him, but others had better reasons to take him down. Still, his name was on the calendar.

Ned's house was a small, neat rambler. I tried the knob, but it was locked.

"That's not a hard lock to pick," José said. "I have something in my car that can open it." He hurried to the car and came back with a small tool. He messed with the lock for a minute, and it opened.

"You know, someday Jett's going to have to arrest us for something like this," I said, entering the house.

José chuckled. "Probably."

We walked through the spotless house, careful not to touch anything. I would almost bet that Ned was the type of person who would notice if anything was moved a fraction of an inch. He had a small office with a computer on a desk. The desk was bigger than the one in his city office.

I moved over and bumped the desk. The computer woke up, and I glanced at the screen. "He left a bank statement up on the computer."

"His own or related to his job?"

My eyes scanned it. "His own, I think." My eyes widened. "Oooo. He wrote a five-thousand-dollar check to someone. His mortgage can't be that high."

José came over and pushed a button with his gloved finger. A copy of the check came up.

I put a hand to my head. "He's paying Macey Newley? That's a lot of money."

"Who is she again?"

"The activist who ties herself to things."

"What would he be paying her for?"

"No idea."

José pointed at the screen. "Look at this. He made a seven-thousand-dollar cash deposit a few days before the murder."

"That's suspicious."

José pulled out his phone and glanced at the screen. "Carrie said Ned just left the diner."

I took out my phone and snapped a picture of the screen. "Let's go." We left the house and rushed to José's car. My mind was spinning. Who would give Ned that much money, and why would he pay Macey? I didn't know if Ned was connected to the mayor's death, but he was definitely up to something.

José held up a paper. It was the missing calendar page.

I grabbed it. "Where did you get this?"

"Ned's garbage."

"Hmm. Ned's looking guilty."

José pulled onto the road. "Or he saw the page and thought it would make him look bad."

"He's guilty of something. What if he paid Macey to go away or something? I don't know if I think he killed the mayor. If he did, it ruins my theory about the mayor's death being connected to the body at Barbra's."

"Why?"

"Ned looks about forty. He probably wasn't alive when Mandy killed Ripley. If he was, he was young."

"It's possible the mayor's and Ripley's deaths aren't connected. Maybe the mayor wanting to develop the land got someone scared enough to look for a body, but they didn't kill the mayor."

"I guess. I wonder where Ned got the seven thousand in cash."

"Now what?"

I sighed. "I have to tell Jett."

He pulled into the diner. "Have fun."

"You don't want to come confess with me?"

"Nope. He'll get less annoyed at you."

I got out of the car and pulled out my phone. It looked like Jett was at his office.

"I'll be back soon," I said. I felt bad about ditching my cinnamon rolls on Anton. "Actually, I might grab a cookie for Jett."

José laughed. "Trying to soften him up?"

I smiled. "It might not work. I give him cookies all the time."

I grabbed a cookie from the diner and hurried to the sheriff's office. I went in and greeted Jane, then knocked on Jett's door and went in. He was standing and shuffling a pile of papers.

"Hey," he said, looking up at me.

"Hello. I brought you a cookie." I held it out, and he arched his eyebrow.

He took it and bit into it. "What did you do?"

"You're so suspicious," I said, holding in a smile.

"You just came to bring me a cookie? I'm not buying it."

"What? I'm not allowed to bring my big, strong, handsome fiancé a cookie?"

He raised his eyebrow.

"Fine. I broke into Ned's office and his house. Oh, and the mayor's office." I would try to leave José out of it.

He sighed. "Stay away from Ned."

"The mayor was meeting with him the day he died."

"I know."

"How?"

"The mayor's wife gave me his electronic planner."

I crossed my arms. "Man. I wanted you to ask how I figured it out so I could brag."

He smiled. "If you broke into the mayor's office, I assume you noticed the missing calendar page and scribbled over the next page to see if there was an indent."

I frowned. "Am I that predictable?"

His smile grew. "Maybe. I know I've seen that trick on *Monk, Murder She Wrote, and CSI*. I figure if Jessica Fletcher did it, you would have it in your head."

"Well, it worked."

"I know you."

"Well, tell me how I figured out that Ned paid Macey five thousand dollars and that he deposited seven thousand dollars just days before the mayor died?"

"Bank statement?"

"Dang it. Why don't you seem surprised?"

"I didn't know about the seven thousand, but I got an order to see Macey's bank statement. She's up to something. I saw the check from Ned."

"And you didn't tell me?"

"Remember how you aren't my boss?" His eyes sparkled. "There are things I shouldn't tell you."

"Ned took the missing calendar page. It was in his garbage."

He rubbed his chin. "Hmm. If he didn't want anyone to see it, then there's something to it. I was planning on talking to him tonight."

"Why would he pay Macey?"

"To get her to back down? I'm not sure. I talked to Macey, but she wasn't cooperative at all. I asked why he gave her the money, and she ignored me. I couldn't stay because I had something, so I need to talk to her again."

"Do you think the mayor knew about the money?"

"I wouldn't be surprised. Maybe he gave the seven thousand to Ned to pay her and do more of his dirty business. It's hard to say."

"Would the mayor want to develop the land so much he would give up all that money?"

"It might not be his money. It could belong to the town. Right now, I'm speculating. I'm still waiting to get permission to check Jepson's accounts. His wife wouldn't show me anything, so I have to go over her head and get a warrant from a judge."

"Did you search the cave?"

"We had some people who specialize in that kind of thing go in. We're still waiting to hear back. We did talk to the bank and look into the money. A man robbed a bank in Wichita forty-five years ago. It was in all the papers. I printed off some copies." He picked up a paper off his desk and handed it to me.

"I should have looked up bank robberies from back then. I could have had Spencer narrow down the dates."

"You have to let me do some things, or I'll get fired," he teased. "The police in Wichita had actually opened a case just the other day. Guess who deposited stolen money? Ned. When Ned deposited the money, the bank thought it was suspicious since some of it was old, so they checked the serial numbers on the money and traced two thousand dollars of it back to the robbery."

"So even if we hadn't figured anything out, Ned would have still looked suspicious."

"Yes. Now we need to figure out how he got that money. Ledford said the spider webs were thick when you went into the cave. That means whoever got the money and gave it to Ned had it for quite a while. I suppose Ned could have gotten it himself, but he's too young to have been involved in anything forty-five years ago. If he got it, someone told him about the cave, or he discovered it on his own. The chances of that are slim. Ned doesn't take me as a spelunker."

"A what?"

"Someone who explores caves."

"Did the mayor give it to him?"

"Maybe the mayor gave him five thousand and someone else gave him two thousand. Or if the money all came from the mayor, maybe someone gave the stolen money to him. He might not have known it was from a robbery."

I nodded. "I need to go back to the diner. Hopefully, the next time I see you, I'll have something to tell you that you don't know."

Jett tilted his head and sighed. "Don't go breaking into places. You already surprised me about the money, remember?"

I smiled. "Yes, but for all the effort I went through today, I thought you would be more surprised by some of the things I found."

He walked around his desk and kissed me. "Don't do anything crazy. I have this under control."

Chapter 11

I cracked an egg and dumped it in a bowl. Creepers meowed around my feet. He loved scrambled eggs and got mad when I only gave him a bite. I cracked a few more and whisked them together. "Hold on," I told him as he clawed at my pants. "I have to cook them."

I had read the newspaper articles Jett printed off for me. They hadn't told me much. A man in a mask had gone in with a gun and stolen fifty thousand dollars. There were no tips, and the police had no leads.

By the time the eggs were ready, Jett had come in and sat at the table. He looked serious.

"Do you want some eggs?" I asked.

"No, thanks."

I gave a small piece to Creepers, and he sniffed it.

Jett leaned back and sighed.

"Is something wrong?" I asked.

"Boyd's fingerprints were in Mayor Jepson's office and also at the construction site."

I grabbed my plate and sat down. "I'm sure there's a reason."

"I can't find him, and he's not answering his phone."

"You know he didn't do it," I said, taking a bite.

"I know, but if it was anyone else, I might wonder."

"You live with him. Wouldn't you know if he left?"

"We don't tell each other when we come and go, and I was already on shift."

"I haven't seen him in a while. Did you try Barbra's?"

"No. I haven't looked hard."

Creepers jumped onto the table to grab more egg off my plate, then jumped on the floor.

"No!" I scolded. "That's naughty. You can't get on the table."

He ignored me and ate the egg.

"That's why I'm a dog person," Jett said, grinning.

"Creepers has never gone to the bathroom on my clothes."

"Conan hasn't done that in a while. I think I can finally declare him potty-trained."

"That's good. I don't want him to stink up my place."

"Do you want to stay here when we get married?"

I shrugged. "It's not important to me. What do you want to do?"

"Your place is smaller than mine but a lot nicer. I think we should sell my house and stay here. Maybe buy a newer house or a condo in a few years."

"What about Conan? He's a yapper. People might hear him down in the diner."

"Boyd's trying to teach him to be quieter."

"I doubt he can be an outside dog. He's too small."

"Nope. You got me a needy dog. He hates to be alone. It's good he has Boyd."

"Do you think Boyd might want to keep him at his place once he gets his condo?"

"Maybe. He's good at entertaining the dog but not so good at the cleanup and stuff. I would have to go over and do that."

I stood and tossed the rest of my eggs. I didn't want Creepers to get too much, and I didn't want to eat anything that touched the cat's mouth.

"Do you want me to help you find Boyd?" I asked.

"If you don't have anything else to do."

"I'll go to Barbra's."

"I should check back at home. He doesn't stay away long unless he's at the diner."

I drove over to Barbra's and pulled into her driveway. Macey Newley was handcuffed to the railing on Barbra's front steps. She sat on the third step and stared at me. I walked past her and knocked on the door.

It cracked open, and Barbra peeked out. "Oh, Ivy. It's you." She pulled the door open and ushered me in. "That environmentalist lady is driving me crazy."

"What's she doing?"

"Protesting the land being developed."

"She can't do that. This is your private property. Do you want me to call Jett? I know he wants to talk to her."

"Maybe later. She's been here all day, and I figure she'll have to go to the bathroom or eat eventually."

"Have you seen Boyd?"

"Not today."

"Jett's been looking for him."

"Why?"

"It's just strange not to know where he is. I better text him to tell him Boyd isn't here." I sent Jett a quick text. "How is the condo coming?"

"Good, good. They put it on hold for a day after the mayor died, but they're working on it again. They say we should be able to move in before Christmas. I was lucky to get in on the first bunch."

"Are you going to be close to Opal?"

"Next door."

"That's really close."

"Yup. I wonder if we'll still be friends in a year. Opal is my best friend, but she might drive me batty, being so close. Still, it'll be nice to be close to so many people. I know I'm close to town, but it might as well be a different planet in the winter. Come sit down."

I paused. "Is someone here?"

"No, why?"

"I thought I heard footsteps."

"It's these old houses. They get you hearing things with all the creaking."

We went into Barbra's living room and sat. Since I'd helped her clean this room out, she'd kept it clean. The first time I came, I couldn't get to the couch. Boxes full of Barbra's things had covered the room.

"Does Jett have an idea who killed the person on my land? It's terrifying to know there's been a dead body on my farm the entire time I've lived here."

"I'm not sure what Jett thinks. I'm pretty sure it was Mandy killing Ripley. It makes a ton of sense."

"I wish I had read the letters now that I know there's a story."

"I wish I'd copied them. Jett had to take them all as evidence."

"There has to be a way to find the girl. Especially if she's Spencer's cousin. He might say he doesn't know, but don't you think he could reach out to some relatives to find out where she ended up?"

"I would think so, but maybe they have a small family. They obviously weren't close if they haven't seen each other for so long."

I heard another noise from upstairs.

Barbra glared at the ceiling, then started telling me about one of her grandchildren in a much louder voice than she usually used.

I was ninety-nine percent sure Boyd was hiding up there. Did he really think I was coming to turn him in? No one would convince me Boyd had killed the mayor. He would have had a hard time climbing up the scaffolding, and he wouldn't have been able to take off the screws and mess with everything with the way he moves.

Barbra ran out of things to say.

"Do you think anyone will run against Boyd now that Jepson is gone?" I asked.

She laughed. "Maybe I should. I could give Boyd a run for his money."

There was a loud thud upstairs.

"Are you hiding a man up there or a horse?" I asked.

"It's just a stray."

I raised my brow and tried not to smile. "A stray lion? It sounded heavy." I stood and walked toward the hall.

"Where are you going?" Barbra asked.

"I'm looking for Boyd." I went down the hall to the stairs. Boyd was awkwardly kneeling halfway up on the stairs with his head stuck between the railing.

"Hey, Ivy," he said like we were passing on the street.

"What are you doing?" Barbra asked with her hands on her hips. "Why would you stick your head in there? Don't you know you're an old man and not a three-year-old?"

He sighed. "I wanted to see who was at the door. I'm stuck good."

"I've never known anyone who gets stuck in as many things as you do," I said, climbing the stairs. I got up higher than him and studied his head. "I don't know how you got in there in the first place."

Barbra shook her head. "These old houses never have the railings close enough together. My kids were always getting stuck. They came out easy enough because they had kid-sized heads, not big melons like Boyd."

"Do you want me to call Jett? He's looking for you anyway."

"No. I'll think of something."

"Why are you hiding?"

He sighed. "Jett left a message on my phone. He said my prints were on some things, and he needed to talk to me. I panicked."

"You know Jett doesn't think you're guilty, right? He just has to ask you the normal questions to clear you. It's part of his job."

Barbra nodded. "That's what I told him."

"So now what?" I asked. "Do we cut it?" The rail was made of wood, so it wouldn't be hard to get through.

"My head or the wood?" Boyd asked.

I ignored him. "We could try butter. That would make a mess."

"This is the dumbest thing I've ever seen you do, Boyd Webster," Barbra said.

I smiled. I'd seen him do things just as bad, but I wouldn't point them out. I pulled out my phone and dialed Jett.

"Hello?" he said. "Did you find him?"

"Yes."

"Good, I was getting scared."

"He got his head stuck in the railing on Barbra's stairs."

"That sounds like Boyd."

"I can hear you!" Boyd said.

Jett laughed. "I'll be right over."

"Macey cuffed herself to Barbra's house."

"That will solve two of my problems. I'll see you in a few minutes."

"Bye." I hung up. "I'm going outside to talk to Macey before Jett gets here, and she clams up."

I went to the porch and sat on the top step. "Hello."

She looked up from her seat just below me. "Hi. Are you going to protest with me?"

"No."

She pushed a curl from her eye. "Then go away."

"This is my friend's house. She wants me here. You're trespassing."

"It's for a good cause."

"All your little protesting is doing is making the woman who lives here nervous. The developers don't see you here, and the mayor's obviously not here. No news crews care you're here. You need to leave."

"Not until they promise not to develop the land."

"Why did Ned give you five thousand dollars? That's a lot of money."

She shifted nervously. "I don't know what you're talking about."

"Yes. You do."

"The sheriff's on his way right now. He's done playing nice. He needs answers."

"He's intimidated by me," she said. "He won't do anything."

"He's busy. The last time he spoke with you, he didn't have time. This time he does, so you might as well tell me why Ned gave you the money."

"Why would I tell you? Don't you run the diner?"

"Yes. You can tell me, and I'll try to help you unless you killed the mayor."

She blinked. "Why would I do that?"

"So he wouldn't develop the land."

"Is that what people think?"

I shrugged. I doubted most people thought about her at all. She wasn't from Muddy Creek.

"I didn't kill him."

"You sure wanted him to leave the land alone."

She frowned. "I... The mayor... I don't know."

"Start over."

"The mayor paid me to come here and protest. I don't normally do protests over something like a farm, but he gave me enough money to make it worth my while. His assistant wrote me a check."

My eyes narrowed. "Why would he want you to protest?"

She shrugged. "Who knows? I don't really care. I just need the money."

"Why are you still here? He's dead."

"I finish what I start. Plus, I really don't think they should develop the area. I usually protest bigger projects, but that doesn't mean these small ones don't matter. Besides, Ned gave me a personal check. It wasn't from the city. He's still around, so I'll finish."

"I don't want you here. You're bothering Barbra, and none of this is her fault. The sheriff will kick you out anyway."

"I know how to get my way with guys like him."

I raised my eyebrow. "Oh?"

"He's an overworked lawman. A little flirting goes a long way with that type."

Jett's truck came into view.

"I wouldn't recommend that," I mused.

"Watch, and I'll teach you how it's done."

"He's not desperate for flirting."

"They all are. They're too busy all the time and don't have time for stuff like that."

I frowned and wondered how often women tried to flirt with Jett to get out of things. Jett wasn't stupid. He wouldn't fall for any of Macey's garbage.

He parked and walked up to us. He took off his sunglasses and looked at Macey. "Are we really going to do this again? How about you get up and leave and go about your business?"

She flashed her white teeth. "Only if the business we have is the same."

I smiled, and Jett shook his head.

"I'm not playing games with you. I have things to do."

She tossed her curls back. "Even a busy sheriff needs to take some time to himself. Buy me a drink and we can discuss the environment."

Jett raised his eyebrow, and I covered my mouth with my hand. I might not be an expert on flirting, but I might be better than Macey.

"Number one, I have a fiancée, and number two, I don't drink or buy drinks for people."

I grinned. "She wants to teach me to flirt and manipulate lawmen. At least that's what she told me."

Jett sighed. "She told you that? How about I arrest her for trespassing, and I'll take you somewhere, and you can flirt with me?"

I stood and walked around Macey and down near Jett. "Normally, I would say yes, but Boyd still has his head stuck."

Macey glared at me.

"Right. I'll arrest her, then help Boyd. Did you try butter?"

"No. That sounds messy."

"Better than tearing up the house."

"True."

Jett held out his hand. "Give me the key to the cuffs."

"No," Macey said.

"How hard do you want this to be?"

"As hard as I can possibly make it."

"You better help Boyd first," I said. "I'm not sure how long he can hold that position."

"Got it. I'll be right back." He pushed past Macey and went into the house.

Macey scowled. "I can't believe you."

"Why?"

"You told the sheriff I was going to flirt with him. Who does that?"

"His fiancée, who doesn't like to see other women flirt with him?"

"He's your fiancé? Why didn't you say that?"

"I don't know you."

"Look, I needed that money. It's not a big deal, okay? People pay me to cause problems sometimes."

"Well, right now isn't the time. The sheriff is working on two murders and doesn't have time for whatever you think you're trying to achieve. The more you interfere, the more it looks like you might be involved."

She took a key from her pocket and opened the handcuffs. She stood and glared at me. "I'll leave for now, but I'm not finished." She stomped off to her car and got in, slamming the door.

I went into the house to see Barbra slathering butter all over Boyd's head. Jett was watching with amusement.

"Macey left," I said.

"Good."

"How often do women try to flirt with you to get out of things?"

"Not often, but it happens. Some people get desperate to get out of tickets."

I grinned at him. "Does it ever work?"

"Sure does," Barbra said. "Every time Jett pulls me over, I just bat my eyes, and he lets me go with a warning."

Jett chuckled. "I don't remember pulling you over more than once."

"But it worked."

I smiled. "What about women under fifty?"

Barbra laughed. "Are you saying I'm not a threat to you?"

Jett went up and pulled on Boyd's head, and it slid through.

"If someone speeds and tries to flirt, I always give them a ticket."

"It's good I don't speed," I said. "I would probably try to flirt with you."

Jett winked. "You do speed, Ivs. You're consistently five over, but I don't usually pull people over for that. I'm actually surprised Ledford's never pulled you over. He's a stickler."

Boyd turned his head from side to side. "I will never do that again. I'm gonna have a kink in my neck for days."

"You better not," Barbra said. "I can't believe you did it the first time. Come on. I'll get you a towel to wipe off the butter." Boyd stood, and she led him down the hall.

"Macey said Ned paid her on command of the mayor to come protest here. She doesn't know why."

Jett nodded. "I bet he wanted her to come make a spectacle of herself so people would think only radicals opposed him. It could help sway the people's opinions to his way of thinking."

"That's a bit extreme."

"He must have really wanted to win."

"Why have Ned pay her?"

"To not leave a trail to him. I bet he gave the money to Ned and had him pay her. That's why it was cash. This would all be easier to figure out if I could get his bank records faster."

"Boyd was hiding here. He thought you might arrest him."

Jett rolled his eyes. "He should know better than that."

"Go tell him that, then I'll speed home, and you can stop me, and I'll see if I can flirt my way out of a ticket."

He grinned. "You better hope I pull you over and not Ledford."

Chapter 12

I was getting a handle on cooking the biscotti. I had to make it in the morning so I could be patient enough to let it cool before I cooked it the second time. I placed it on the island to cool, then I hurried over to teach my Zumba class.

"We thought you were lost," Barbra said when I entered.

"Sorry. I'm making biscotti. You should all come over a few hours after Zumba, and I'll give you a piece."

"Sounds good to me," Opal said, pulling her sweatband over her curly gray hair. "I haven't tried anything new in a while."

Barbra looked around. "If we all meet at the same time, I can tell you all about how Boyd got his head stuck in my stair railing yesterday."

Everyone laughed, even Boyd.

"Is everyone ready?" I asked, flipping on the music. Since most of my class was over sixty, we only danced to the oldies. I was beginning to feel like Richard Simmons, but it was what they liked.

After class, I hurried home for a quick shower and to spend a few minutes with Creepers. He didn't seem overly thrilled with my attention, so I went back to the kitchen and cut the biscotti. I placed the slices on a baking sheet and slid them into the oven.

By the time the cooks came in, the biscotti was already finished and cooling for the second time.

José looked at it. "You're getting better at it. You must have gotten up early."

"Extra early. It's a Zumba day."

"What did Jett say about our little outing?"

Jett stood in the kitchen door. "José was with you?"

José swallowed hard.

"I didn't tell him you were with me."

Jett sighed. "I'd rather you were with her, to be honest. It's safer. Still, couldn't you try talking her out of these things?"

I grinned. "You think that would work?"

"Not really. Good news, though. Records at the city show that Boyd visited with the mayor a few days before he died, just like Boyd said. People could also vouch that he had gone to the construction site to talk about buying a condo."

I was relieved. "Have you told him?"

"Yep. He's feeling better. He's out right now, taking Conan on a walk."

"Do you want to try my biscotti?" I asked. "It's better this time."

He looked down at the platter. "Sure."

"It's better if you dip it in some kind of liquid. I've only tried hot chocolate."

He took a bite. "It reminds me of something."

"I'll make you some cocoa so you can try it that way."

"I found something out," José said. "Well, Carrie told me something. She said that Kara Wilson's parents were good friends with Spencer Cunningham's parents. Kara's about Carrie's age, and they talk a lot."

I grabbed a mug and filled it with hot water. "Kara's younger than Spencer."

"Yeah, but Kara told Carrie that something happened between her parents and the Cunninghams back when the Cunninghams were staying on Barbra's farm. Her parents did a huge favor for them. Something that always bothered them. Kara didn't know what it was, but they told her to stay away from that property."

"That's odd," I said, handing Jett his hot cocoa. "Her parents are still alive, right?"

"Yes. They live in Wichita."

"Kara wants to buy the property."

José nodded. "She said her parents want her to buy it. They're willing to pay more than it's worth."

Anton and Livy came in the back door and grabbed aprons.

Jett dipped his biscotti in his mug and took a bite. "How good of friends were they? Good enough to help their neighbors bury a body?"

Anton sighed as he pulled on his hairnet. "Why is it always a body with you people? Why can't I ever walk in here and hear a conversation about the Kansas City Chiefs?"

I smiled at him. "I'm not into basketball."

Anton looked at Jett. "She's hurting me."

Jett laughed. "The Kansas City Chiefs are a football team."

"Oh. Well, I'm obviously not into football either."

Anton shook his head. "Just bodies. It's always bodies. I'm even willing to talk about *The Bachelor*."

Livy smiled. "I never miss an episode." She grabbed her notepad and disappeared into the dining area.

I turned to José. "Does Carrie know where Kara's parents live?"

"I'm not sure. She won't be in today, but I can text her."

"Do not go talk to them," Jett said. "I'll handle it."

I nodded. I hadn't had time to think about what I wanted to do. "So Kara doesn't want Barbra's land. It's for her parents? If Kara doesn't know what her parents did, she probably wouldn't kill the mayor over the land. Not unless she isn't telling you something."

"What?" Jett asked. I'd been muttering to myself.

"Just thinking."

Jett took another piece of biscotti. "I'm not sure I would pass over a cookie for this stuff, but it's not bad."

"I just wanted to make it because it sounded cool."

"The first time you told me about it, I thought it was a type of pasta."

"Next time, I'll try it with almonds."

Jett's phone rang, and he excused himself and went into José's office to take the call. I arranged the biscotti to look neater, so it would be ready when Barbra and all the other Zumba ladies came in.

A few minutes later, Jett came out smiling. "I have something you'll want to hear."

"Oh?"

"The forensics team working on the cave found something."

My eyes lit up with excitement. "What?"

"They found some papers. One had a name, an address, and a phone number. Ripley Higgins."

I smiled. "A last name. What's the address and phone number?"

He held up a sticky note. "I'm not sure it will help you if he died forty-five years ago."

"He might still have family there."

"It's possible." I copied down the address and phone number, then ran upstairs. I shut myself in my apartment and looked down at the number. There wasn't a lot of chance the phone number was still good.

I pulled out my phone and typed it in. It rang twice, and a woman answered.

"Hello?"

"Hi," I said. "I'm calling about Ripley Higgins?"

"Oh. Let me give you a better number."

I frowned. "A better number?"

"We get calls for that family all the time. I think they write their old number on things so they won't get solicitors. I finally hunted them down so people will stop calling me. Are you ready?"

I grabbed my pencil. "Yes." She gave me a number, and I copied it down.

"When you talk to them, tell them to quit giving people this number."

"I will, thanks."

I hung up and tried the new number. It rang, and right as I was about to hang up, a woman answered. "Hello, this is Mandy."

Mandy? I froze. It couldn't be the same one. She wouldn't kill Ripley, then be connected to his phone number.

"Hello?" she said when I didn't respond.

"Mandy Cunningham?"

It was quiet for a moment. "Who is this?"

"Sorry. My name is Ivy. I was cleaning out a house in Muddy Creek. I found some letters that I think belong to you. At least if you're Mandy Cunningham."

"You found my letters? I've thought about them so many times. I can't believe I left them behind."

"Can I bring them to you?"

"I live in Topeka. That's over a two-hour drive."

"I know how important letters can be. I don't mind bringing them."

"Can I come to you?"

"Sure."

"Can you meet me tomorrow?"

"Of course. Do you want to meet me at Sue's Diner?"

"It's still there?"

"Yes, I own it."

"How crowded is it? I don't want to run into anyone I knew when I was there."

"I live above the diner. We can meet there if you want."

"That would be great."

"There's an entrance around the back."

"I'll be there at noon."

I hung up and smiled. I rushed down to the diner. Jett was in José's office again on his phone. When I saw him put it in his pocket, I rushed in.

"I found Mandy!" I told him. "I'm not sure why, but the people at the number you gave me gave me her number."

"That's really weird. Why would someone at Ripley's number know where Mandy was?"

"I have no idea."

"That's not the only strange thing," he said. "The body from Barbra's land has been identified by his dental records. It belonged to a man named Richard Marks, not Ripley Higgins."

"What?" My head couldn't wrap around that.

"It starts with an R."

"So Mandy killed Richard Marks? The letters were from him?"

"That's what it looks like."

"Then who is Ripley Higgins?"

"No idea."

"Could there have been three drifters? The letter in the cave was to Ripley, and it talked about the girl. I'm so confused. Could Mandy have killed Richard, then gone off with his friend?"

"What other explanation could there be?" Jett asked. "It's strange that a phone number could connect to her after all these years."

"I won't be able to sleep tonight. My mind will go crazy."

"Maybe the letters were from Richard, but Mandy liked Ripley? Only one letter was written by Mandy, so who knows what her feelings were?"

I shook my head. "Her letter said she loved him and he was everything to her."

"Maybe the letters to her were from Richard, but hers was to Ripley."

"No. That would still make Ripley the dead one."

"Right. I have no idea. Maybe they were from Ripley, and hers was to Richard."

I smiled slightly. "I was a lot less confused before you started speculating."

Jett grinned. "Sorry. I usually pace around my house talking to myself like that until something makes sense."

My smile slipped. "Mandy's coming tomorrow to get the letters, but I no longer have them."

"I can give them back. I think we've gotten everything we can from them. We couldn't get any clear prints, and I have copies of them."

"Thanks."

"Where are you meeting her?"

"In my apartment."

"I don't want you alone."

"She didn't want to risk running into anyone she knew here. She might not talk to me if I have someone with me."

"I don't trust someone we know is a killer. I'll hide in the kitchen so I can hear."

"If she finds out, she might get angry."

"If you accuse her of murder, she'll also be angry."

"Why would I accuse her right out?"

Jett raised his brow. "I know you, Ivs. There's about a fifty percent chance you will. I'll stay quiet in the kitchen.

I won't come out unless you need me. I will have to talk to her eventually, but I can do that after she leaves. I'll run down to the diner and catch her."

"Okay. This is exciting! We're going to figure something out."

"Maybe. You might be too tired tomorrow from staying up all night trying to figure this out."

"Probably. Do you do that?"

"What?"

"Stay up all night trying to figure out cases?"

He shrugged. "Not usually. I do sometimes, but I've gotten good at turning off my brain at night. When I first got the job, it was harder."

José poked his head in. "What are you two up to?"

"Just talking," I said.

"That's good. I don't want anything questionable going on in my office."

"Ha ha. Do you want to know what we found out?"

José came in and shut the door. "You know it."

Chapter 13

I paced across my living room floor and waited for Mandy to arrive. I made Jett go into the kitchen ten minutes before she should arrive, just in case she came early. I didn't want her hearing voices inside. Creepers was asleep in my room, so I closed the door so he wouldn't come out and interrupt. I needed time to think.

Footsteps on the stairs outside made me pause. That had to be her. There was a knock, and I opened the door to find a couple in their sixties. She looked short standing next to him.

I smiled. "Hi, you must be Mandy. I'm Ivy." I held out my hand, and she shook it.

"I'm Mandy, and this is my husband, Ripley."

As I shook his hand, I tried not to let my eyes bug out of my head. "Come in and have a seat." They entered and sat on the couch. I took a seat on my recliner and grabbed the letters from the side table.

Mandy smiled as her eyes fell on them. She pushed a piece of shoulder-length brown hair behind her ear. "I've kicked myself so many times for leaving my letters behind."

I handed them to her. "Sorry I read them. I figured the people they belonged to weren't alive anymore."

She grinned at her husband. "I'm fine with it. I didn't write them."

Ripley smiled and ran a hand over his thin gray hair. "I don't remember what I wrote, but I was a young idiot back then, so I'm sure they were awful."

"There is one written by you," I said. "It was sealed."

Mandy pulled the bottom letter from the pile and glared at it.

"Do I get to read it now?" Ripley asked.

She shook her head. "Nope. I was steaming mad when I wrote that. I've always been glad you never saw it."

He nodded. "You had every reason to be mad."

I pressed my lips together as I tried to decide what to say. I was coming up blank.

"I wasn't just mad."

"I know. I remember you yelling at me. You've never yelled at me like that since. I'm still scared to remember it."

She patted his hand. "We're past it."

I fidgeted with my ring. "The last letter said you killed him."

She opened it, and her eyes scanned it. Ripley read it over her shoulder and frowned. "I thought I did. Not literally, of course. The look on his face... It was awful."

He squeezed her hand.

I took a deep breath. "I'm sorry to be so nosy, but can you tell me your story? I've been making it up in my head from the letters, but I honestly thought you killed him."

She smiled at Ripley. "It's good you didn't disappear, or things would look bad for me."

He chuckled. "It sure would. It looks like a murder confession."

Mandy turned to me. "I went one summer to stay with my aunt and uncle. They were strict and didn't want me to interact with the people in town, but they would let me go on walks. I didn't mind. I'm a bit of an introvert, and I could spend the days happily reading. One day on my walk, I met Ripley."

"Best day of my life," he said.

"He was passing through town with his friend."

"Trevor?" I asked.

"Yes."

"I got that from the letters. Was there only two of you?"

"Yep," Ripley said. "We were out to see the country. After I met Mandy, my priorities shifted. We started meeting in secret and leaving letters in a tree."

"And your friend didn't like that?"

"Not at all. He wanted to keep moving, but I wanted to stay to see if Mandy would leave with me eventually."

Mandy nodded. "I had to keep it a secret from my aunt and uncle."

"Trevor was getting antsy," Ripley said. "We were staying in a cave we found. I shouldn't admit this, but Trevor was stealing things from the people in the town. I knew about it because it was a lot of stuff. He wanted to go to a nearby town to sell it, but I wasn't in a hurry. He kept stealing more. Trevor robbed a bank in Wichita. At least he bragged he did. I never knew if it was true."

I leaned forward. "And you didn't tell anyone?"

"No. Trevor was older than me and had a temper. I was scared to make him mad."

I needed to find Trevor. What if he was the one who killed Richard Marks?

"My uncle found out about us," Mandy explained. "He was livid. I had to sneak out at night. One day, my cousin Spencer cornered me. He told me two drifters had been stealing from the town, and they were planning to steal from our family. He told me the only reason Ripley was talking to me was so he could get close enough to steal from us.

"To say I was angry is an understatement. I found Ripley that night and yelled at him. I didn't let him get a word in." She looked down at the letters and frowned. "He looked so upset. He had tears in his eyes. I ran home and wrote that letter. Two days later, I got his letter begging to talk to me. I went, and he explained everything."

"And you believed him?" I asked.

"Yes."

"What happened to Trevor?"

Ripley leaned back. "He was mad that I wouldn't let Mandy go. I asked him to deliver a letter after Mandy got angry with me. He said that was the end of it. We fought. He said he would deliver the letter, and then he was never helping me again. He left without me. I never saw him again."

"Have you ever tried to find him?"

"No. He was mad, and I was finished with that relationship."

"He didn't take the things from the cave."

Ripley raised his eyebrow. "How do you know about that?"

"I've been in the cave."

"I thought Trevor would have cleaned it out. It had a lot of stuff he could make money from."

"Do you know what Trevor's last name was?"

Ripley smiled. "You've turned into a detective over the letters?"

I shrugged. "It's been like a puzzle for me."

"Trevor's name wasn't even Trevor."

A chill ran across my body. "It was Richard Marks."

Ripley's eyes widened. "Yes. I'm impressed. How did you discover that?"

I rubbed my arms to get rid of the goose bumps. "The farm Mandy was staying at. A body was discovered there recently. It was a man named Richard Marks."

Ripley and Mandy shared a concerned look.

"Wow," he said. "What could have happened?"

"I don't know. The body wasn't found until after I found the letters. For a while, I believed the body was Ripley and that Mandy killed him."

Ripley laughed softly. "Mandy wouldn't hurt a fly. How was the body found?"

"The mayor was recently murdered. He wanted to develop the farmland, and someone began digging around trees. The police think the murderer didn't want the land developed because the body might be found. Did Trevor have enemies in town?"

Ripley shook his head. "He kept on the down-low. I don't think most people knew we were in town because we stayed in the cave."

"Did anyone else know about the cave?"

"Not that I know of."

"Someone's been going to the cave. Probably not a lot, but there was a lot of money in the cave, and the dust wasn't as heavy on the case it was in. Someone's been slowly taking money."

His eyes narrowed. "Interesting. Someone must have found it. How did you?"

"There was a watch near Trevor's body. It had the cave's location scratched onto it."

"And the police know all of this?" Mandy asked.

I nodded.

"So they should be able to solve it?"

"I hope so."

She bit her lip. "I wonder if my uncle did it. If so, it's partially my fault."

"Was he violent?"

"Well, he wasn't nice. I never saw him hurt anyone, but he was angry when he found out about Ripley. He'd never met him. What if he saw Trevor deliver the last letter? He might have mistaken him for Ripley."

"But what about the missing money?" Ripley asked. "He wouldn't know where the cave was to take any."

"Maybe he saw the watch when he was burying him," I suggested.

"That could be. Have the police cleaned it all out?"

"I think so."

He sighed. "I bet there's stuff in there that points at me since I was staying there."

Mandy put a hand to her chest. "You won't get in trouble, will you?"

"It's possible. I did know Trevor was stealing, and I didn't do anything to stop him. It might look like I was in on it. That might make me look like a suspect in his killing as well."

"No," she muttered. "This can't be happening."

I swallowed. Now I felt guilty. I didn't want Ripley to get into trouble. "I doubt you'll be a suspect. Whoever killed Trevor is probably the same person who killed the mayor."

"That would mean it wasn't my uncle," Mandy said. "He's been dead for a while. Unless he killed him and had someone help him dispose of the body."

"Did you know the people who owned the farm behind your uncle?"

"No. I didn't know most people from town. It was awkward being here. I met some people, but I felt like an outsider. That's why I don't want to run into anyone I might have met. I also don't want to see my cousin. It's been years."

I couldn't help thinking that maybe Kara's parents had helped Mandy's uncle bury the body. That could be the secret they didn't tell Kara and why they wanted to buy the farm.

"I think you two need to tell the sheriff everything you know. It could help in his investigation."

Ripley nodded and played with his neon-green keychain. "I'm sure he'll be looking for us soon if we don't. Do you know where we can find him?"

"He's probably in the diner. Do you want me to walk you down?"

"Yes, thank you."

I opened the door and waited for them to exit, then we made our way down the steps. I deliberately walked slowly so Jett would have time to go through my bedroom and down into the diner.

We went in the front doors and found Jett sitting at a booth. He didn't look like someone who had just run down the stairs. Now, he was going to have to pretend he hadn't heard the entire conversation already.

"This is Sheriff Malone," I told them. "Sheriff, this is Mandy and Ripley Higgins. They need to talk to you."

"Take a seat," he said. "Order some food."

"Will you stay with us?" Mandy asked me.

"If you want me to."

Mandy and Ripley sat across from Jett, and I sat beside him. They ordered food, and Jett waited patiently while they ate. When they finished, they told him the same thing they told me. Jett did a good job of pretending he hadn't already heard it.

"Have you talked to Spencer since that summer?" he asked.

"No," Mandy said, looking at her napkin. "I don't know anything that happened with the family after I left. I cut all ties and never looked back."

Jett asked a few more questions, then they left.

"What do you think?" I asked.

Jett took a bite of his pie. "I'm not sure. Mandy's lying about something."

"Why do you think that?"

"She wouldn't make eye contact, and she kept fidgeting."

"She's an introvert. Isn't that normal?"

"Maybe. But she also said she's had no contact with her family since that summer. If that's true, how did she know her uncle died?"

"A guess? He would be pretty old if he was still alive."

"That could be. I feel like she's hiding something."

"Why don't I feel that way?" I asked. I always assume people are hiding things, but it hadn't crossed my mind when I talked to Mandy.

Jett smiled. "Because you're enthralled in the love story. You want Mandy and Ripley to have the happily ever after you were looking for in the letters."

I frowned. He might be right. "I don't think they could have killed the mayor. How would they stage that and get the mayor to go up there? I don't see it."

"I'm not saying they killed the mayor. One of them might have killed Trevor... Richard. I'm not only looking into the murders as being connected. It's possible the mayor was killed for something completely unrelated."

"What about the holes in Barbra's land?"

"I would guess the person who killed Richard did that, but that doesn't mean they killed Jepson."

"I guess not. Is the cave completely cleaned out?"

"No. The valuable stuff is, and forensics went through everything. I need to go to Wichita and talk to Kara's parents. They must know something."

"I wish I could go with you."

"You could if you were my deputy."

I smiled. "That's not going to happen."

"Nope. I guess I'll take Ledford."

Chapter 14

I placed a tray of desserts on the table in the party room. Barbra's book club was meeting soon, and I wanted to make sure they had everything they needed. I wanted to go back to the cave. I didn't think I would find anything important, not after forensics had been there, but something there might give me a clue.

Jett was talking to Kara's parents in Wichita, so I figured today was my best chance at getting another look. Even if he saw my location, he wouldn't be able to get back in time to stop me. Once I had the book club settled, I would head over there.

"I'm glad you let us do book club here," Barbra said, placing a book at the head of a table. Her purple hair was pulled back into a ponytail today. "It's nicer than any other place we've done it."

"I'm glad you can use it." I smiled. "Besides, you all buy enough desserts to make it worth it. What book are you talking about today?"

"*Little Women.* Have you read it?"

"In high school. I bet Boyd loved that choice."

Barbra laughed. "Not at all. Serves him right for never coming to the meeting when we vote on what we're reading for the year."

"I still can't believe you hid Boyd from me the other day."

She took a deep breath. "I know, I know. He came pounding on my door in a panic."

"I can't believe he thought Jett might arrest him."

"Arrest who?" Boyd asked, entering the room. "Hopefully arrest whoever chose that stupid book for the month."

Barbra laughed. "You didn't like it?"

"Not at all. I hated the entire book. It wouldn't have been so bad if it wasn't so big. It made me cry twice."

"But it had a good love story," Barbra said.

"Nope. People ended up with the wrong people."

"Maybe next time you'll come and help us choose the books for the year."

"It's not worth my time to be there. I get outvoted on everything I suggest. I might start my own book club. I'll call it *The book club for people who don't want to read boring, stupid books.*"

Barbra grinned. "Good luck finding members."

"I have to go," I said. "Let José know if you need any-thing."

"Where are you off to?" Boyd asked.

I shrugged. "I just need to go check something."

"What?"

"I need to look for something."

"Stop giving me the Jett treatment."

I laughed. "What's the Jett treatment?"

"It's when you're about to do something you know Jett doesn't want you to do, so you try to say something that isn't a lie but doesn't actually explain anything either."

Barbra laughed. "He's got you figured out."

I scowled. "I think you're right."

"So what are you doing?" he asked.

"I'm going to the cave."

"Why? There's not going to be anything new."

"I want to see if I missed anything. Ever since I talked to Mandy and Ripley, I'm more confused than ever. I know the forensics team would have taken anything important, but I don't have anything else I can think to do."

"Don't go into a cave alone," Barbra commanded. "I'm still bothered that there was a body on my land. I don't need you getting hurt."

"I'll be careful."

"I'll come," Boyd offered.

"It'll be too hard for you," I pointed out.

"But if you have a little slip, no one will know, and you'll be all alone and hurt."

"I have my phone, and you know where I am. If I'm not back in a few hours, you can tell Jett."

"You could be dead in a few hours."

I rolled my eyes. "I'll text you when I get there. I probably won't be able to when I'm in the cave, but I'll try."

"I'll give you thirty minutes between texts. Anything longer and I send someone."

"Alright." I was going to have to hurry.

I grabbed everything I needed and drove to the cave. I was sad I was missing Opal and Boyd arguing about the book, but this was the time I had. I couldn't swear the two would argue, but that was usually how it went. I sometimes wondered if they had opposing views just so they could fight about things.

The cave had cones around it and crime scene tape connecting them. The rocks covering the entrance were off to the side. I stepped over the tape and sat at the mouth of the cave. I sent a text to Boyd telling him I was here. I switched on my headlamp and slid inside. Going down the second time wasn't as difficult because I knew what to expect.

I'd worn a jacket so I wouldn't freeze like last time. I stood when I got to the bottom of the slope and glanced around. The cool air hit my face, and I took a moment to admire the beautiful cavern. Since I only had thirty minutes before Boyd would panic, I hurried through the cave and into the cavern full of things Trevor... Richard had stolen.

There was still a lot. It made sense since whoever took it out would have to crawl. Forensics probably only took things of interest. With only my headlight, the cave was too dark. Every sound made me jump, and the eerie shadows made my skin crawl.

I turned my phone light on to give me more light. There wasn't anything worth disturbing. I made my way back out of this area to the main area. I looked up at the cave entrance, and my eyes went wide. A man's legs were dangling into the opening. The legs and shoes didn't look familiar.

I backed up to the side until I touched the cold cave wall, and I flipped off all my lights. I wasn't sure what I would do if they got down and shined a light on me, which was likely. I moved along the wall, hoping to come to a crevice or somewhere I could get behind. The wall turned without warning, and I almost slipped. I went around a corner and kept going. How had I not noticed another path when I'd been in here twice? Thick spiderwebs hit my face, and I shivered.

I kept going and wondered where I would end up. My phone light was all I dared to use, so I flipped it on. I was in a tight pathway. There were only a few inches from me to the other wall. I kept going, hoping whoever entered the cave wouldn't come this way. Since neither Ledford nor I saw it last time, it was probably more obvious to go the other way. I wondered if forensics had discovered it. My guess was they hadn't. If they had, the spiderwebs wouldn't be so thick.

When I got to the end of the path, it opened up into a ten-by-ten cavern. I shined my light around and noticed a small crack, probably big enough to get behind. I hurried over and stuffed myself inside and around a small corner. I wasn't sure whether it would hide me or if part of me would show.

Footsteps sounded in the hallway I'd just come from. This was just great. With my luck, Boyd told someone, and it would be someone I knew. A light shone into the area, and I pressed closer into the crevice. I closed my eyes and tried not to think of how many spiders could be crawling over me at this very moment.

I heard someone mutter to themselves. I opened my eyes and peeked out. The man was holding a flashlight, and he was dressed in black. With such dim light, I wouldn't recognize him even if I knew him.

I pressed back again and hoped he would move on. Steps came closer to me, and I took shaky breaths. I hoped they couldn't be heard. A hand touched my arm, and I screamed. The person yelled and jerked back. I jumped out and pulled my arm back, ready to punch.

The man turned and fled. I flipped on my headlamp and chased him. He flew through the narrow hallway and was up the slope and out before I could get a good look at him.

I started up the slope, and the opening went dark. He'd covered it with something.

"Don't panic," I whispered. The worst thing that could happen was I would be stuck here until Boyd told someone. I climbed up the slope and pushed the rock covering the opening. It didn't budge, and my shoes kept slipping. He must have piled it up fast. I slid back down and took a few breaths.

I might as well explore the cavern I'd found. This time, I shined my light all around the walls and floor as I walked down the hallway. That man had to have been here for a reason. I was almost sure no one had been here in a long time. There was no way spiders could make such impressive webs so fast—At least I hoped they couldn't do it that fast.

Something on the ground caught my eye. I shined my light on it and frowned. It was a green keychain. Ripley. He'd been down here, but why? He must have been looking for something. I picked it up and put it in my pocket. If Ripley realized he left it, he might be back.

I went into the cavern and back over to my hiding spot. Ripley had stuck his arm in there. Was there something I didn't notice? I shined my light into the crevice and let it illuminate each space. I got to my knees and felt around. There were lots of small crevices where something could be hidden in. I pictured a scorpion popping out and stinging me.

My fingers brushed something, and I pulled out a small velvet box covered in thick dust. Getting distracted in here could be a bad thing, so I stuck the box in my jacket pocket. I wasn't sure what it was, but I bet Ripley was looking for it.

"Ivy!" José's voice echoed through the cave.

"Coming!" I yelled back. I rushed to the main cavern and found José looking into the cave from above.

"Can you get out?" he asked.

"Yes." I climbed up the slope and out of the cave. I sat on the ground to catch my breath. "Did Boyd send you?"

"Yes. He told me right after you left. I had to finish something, then I hurried over. Someone blocked the opening."

"I'm almost sure it was Ripley. He was down there looking for something." I pulled the box out of my pocket and blew on it. I thought the dust would scatter, but it was too thick to even be disturbed. I pried the box open and looked down at a heart-shaped locket. It had an M on it.

"Let's get back to the diner, and you can call Jett."

"Why call him? He'll be back soon."

"Yes, but someone tried to trap you in a cave. That means they might mean you harm."

"I scared him. Well, he scared me, then I scared him. He might have acted without thinking."

"It's still dangerous. Come on. I'll follow you back." He reached out a hand and helped pull me up.

I brushed off my pants. "Do I have any bugs in my hair?"

His eyes scanned my head. "You have a lot of stuff in your hair. Nothing moving that I can see."

I drove home with José behind me. When I got to the diner, I saw Jett's truck. I hopped out of my car and hurried into the diner. No Jett. I found him in the kitchen, sitting at the island talking to Anton.

"Hey," I said.

"What happened to you?" he asked, standing.

I touched my hair. "Let's go upstairs."

We went up to my living room, and he sat on the couch. I went to sit next to him, and he raised his eyebrow. "You probably don't want to sit here. Your clothes are filthy."

"Right. I went back to the cave."

He closed his eyes. "Ivy..."

"I know. I wanted to see if anything was missed."

"Forensics is thorough."

"I found this." I handed him the box with the locket. "It was in a different area than all the other stuff."

He opened it and studied the locket.

"Someone came in when I was there. They covered the hole so I couldn't get out, but José came and let me out."

He looked at me with a serious expression. "I don't want you to go in the cave again. Crime tape means you stay out."

I decided to ignore him. "The person dropped this." I handed him the keychain.

He frowned and took it. "I saw Ripley with this."

"I bet the locket was for Mandy. Or it belonged to her."

"I need to talk to them."

"Be careful."

Chapter 15

The next day, I stood in the sheriff's office looking for Jett. The only person I could see in the office was a young woman in charge of... well, I wasn't sure what she was in charge of. I'd seen her in here a few times, but I have no idea what her job title was. She was around twenty-five and always had a file in her hand when I saw her.

The door opened behind me, and Jane came in. "Hi, Ivy." She took off her jacket and walked past me, draping the jacket over her chair. She sat at her desk and made sure her brown hair wasn't messed up.

"I came too early," I told her. "I was hoping to run into Jett."

"I didn't see him outside. He's not usually here this early. He goes around to check on the town before he comes here."

"I can track his phone, but he turns off the tracking sometimes when he needs to do something he doesn't want me messing in."

Jane laughed and straightened her glasses. "I can see why someone dating you might do that."

I smiled. "Yeah, I'm nosy."

"And because of that, a lot of cases have been solved. You should go to the police academy."

"I would be horrible at all the physical stuff."

"I just saw Ned Forshaw putting luggage in a car. I was going to text the sheriff to let him know."

"Really? He's a suspect."

"That's why I was going to text him."

"I'm going to see if he's still there."

"I'll come with you. Lyla, watch my desk."

The woman, who must be Lyla, looked up from a filing cabinet and nodded.

Jane and I jumped into my car, and I hurried to Ned's house.

"What does Lyla do?" I asked.

"Whatever needs doing. I'm not sure about her job title. She grabs donuts, files papers, and does anything else anyone in the office needs."

"That sounds like a terrible job."

"I think she enjoys it."

We pulled up to Ned's house. The trunk of his white car was open. He came out of the front door with a box in his hands. We got out, and his eyes went wide. He rushed to the trunk, put the box in, then tried to get in the passenger side. The door was locked. He pulled the handle a few times, like an impatient toddler, then turned and ran.

Jane and I shared a look, then we tore off after him. He ran around his house and into the trees behind. One thing I'd learned in Kansas was that there was a lot of space. Where I came from, if you ran in one direction, you'd come to another house soon. Not here. He could run for days and never come to anything. Back here looked like a massive forest.

I might not be in great shape, but we were already gaining on Ned. Jane was ahead of me, which wasn't surprising. She used to be a cop but came here to be a secretary and lead a quieter life. So much for that.

Jane was one of those people who looked good wearing a pantsuit and no make-up. Her hair was always in place but not fancy, and her eyelashes were dark and long without mascara. I wondered what Ledford thought of her. She was probably in her early forties, which was about the age I placed Ledford.

I shook my head. It wasn't time to play matchmaker. I might have a better relationship with Ledford than I did a month ago, but that didn't mean I would wish him on Jane.

Ned ran around the trees. I wasn't sure if he was trying to lose us or confuse us, but all it did was make him slower.

Jane lunged forward and knocked Ned to the ground. I stopped and tried to get my breathing under control. Ned tried to escape, but Jane had a good grip on him. She twisted him around and sat on his back. He tried to get up, but she slammed him back to the earth. Pulling his arms behind him, she cuffed him.

"You still carry handcuffs?" I asked her. I was fairly confident she wasn't allowed to arrest people anymore.

She grinned up at me. "It's a good thing, isn't it?" She got to her feet and brushed off her pants. Ned rolled over and sat up. "Stay down there," Jane said.

He glared at her. "You aren't a cop. You can't arrest me."

"Why were you skipping town?" I asked.

"Who says I was?"

"Why did you run?"

He took a deep breath. "I know all about you, Miss Clark. Always solving mysteries. It drove the mayor crazy. I figure if you're focused on me, I want to be somewhere else. I know you were in my house."

"Why run if you aren't guilty of anything?" I asked even though I wanted to ask how he knew I'd been there.

"I didn't kill the mayor."

"No one said you did."

"But you think I did, and so does the sheriff."

I tilted my head. "How do you know what I'm thinking?"

"I'll call the sheriff," Jane said, walking a short distance away. "Kick him if he tries to get up."

"Look, someone set me up. I know it looks bad," he said.

"Set you up how?" I asked.

He just stared at me.

"Why did you pay Macey Newley five thousand dollars?"

His eyes narrowed. "Who says I did?"

"Your bank statement and Macey."

"The mayor wanted her to come here. It had nothing to do with me. He just made me pay her."

"Why would he want her to come oppose him?"

"To get attention. What else? If she brought enough attention to herself and made herself look a little crazy, it made the mayor and his plans look better. He would appear to be the sensible one."

"You deposited seven thousand dollars. What did you do with the other two thousand?"

"That's none of your business."

Jane came back. "The sheriff's on his way."

"You kept the money? Were you supposed to give it all to Macey?"

He shrugged.

"The mayor was meeting you the day he died."

Ned pressed his lips together.

"Did you meet him?"

He glared at me and didn't say anything.

I took a step toward him, and his eyes widened. "Okay! I met him at the construction site."

Ned was a pushover. I leaned down and rested my hands on my knees. He flinched. That was the mayor's assistant I'd seen in action.

"Why are you flinching? You think I'm going to hit you or something?"

"How should I know?" he muttered.

"Why were you at the construction site?"

He frowned. "Jepson was meeting someone there. He made me come. He told me to meet him in front of the area. I didn't want to. It was so early. I met him, and he wanted to see everything to make sure the workers were doing a quality job. He climbed up the scaffolding, and he fell."

"And you ran and jumped the fence?"

"I panicked."

I stood tall and looked at Jane. She shrugged. If Ned was telling the truth, the rigged scaffolding might not have been meant for the mayor. I wondered who would have been the first person to stand there in the morning if the mayor hadn't done it first.

"You didn't like the mayor," I stated. It was obvious to anyone who saw Mayor Jepson boss Ned around.

"No one did. I'm not guilty for that. Tons of people hated him worse than I did."

"Who was he supposed to meet at the site?"

"I don't know."

"You didn't see anyone?"

He looked up at the sky. "No."

"He's lying," Jane said. "I can spot a liar a mile away."

"Who did you see?" I asked.

He swallowed. "I'm not talking to you anymore."

Jett came running through the trees. "What's going on?" he asked.

Jane gave him a quick recap, and Jett pulled Ned to his feet.

"Let's go talk at the station," Jett said. "Walk." He nudged Ned gently in the direction he needed to go.

"Your secretary isn't allowed to handcuff people," Ned muttered.

"Keep walking."

Jane smiled as we walked back to the car. "I miss being a cop sometimes."

"Do you think you'll go back?" I asked.

"No. It's too much stress."

"I have some cookies at the diner. Do you want to come have one?" I'm not great at making friends, but I was sure Jane and I could be friends.

"I would, but I need to get back to work. Your cookies are delicious."

"I'll bring you some."

"Thanks. If you ever need a favor, I'm here for you."

I tried to keep a straight face. "What do you think about Ledford?"

She raised her eyebrow. "In what sense? He's unpleasant for the most part. Not as bad as when I first came."

"He grows on you," I said. "I wanted him to leave when he first came, but now I don't mind him so much."

"He'd probably be less tolerable if he wasn't good-looking."

I wrinkled my nose. "You think he's good-looking?"

"Sure. I mean, the mustache is a little much. But he's tall and strong."

"Tall? He's only as tall as I am." I'm five-foot-five if I stand straight, and I look Ledford in the eye.

"Well, compared to me, he's tall."

I smiled. Maybe there could be something between the two of them.

"Don't smile like that. His personality isn't my style."

❧

"Wow, José. This looks great." I wasn't exaggerating. The gooey cheese on the noodles made my mouth water.

"Do you want a scoop?" he asked.

"Yes, please."

He handed me a plate, and I sat at the island in the diner. I took a bite. "It's sooo good." José experiments in the kitchen when we have slow days. Tuesday used to be the slowest day, but word got out that José was making new things, and dinner became a popular time.

"The dining room is loaded," Anton said. "Maybe José should do his experiments every day."

José shook his head. "Then it wouldn't be special, and people would stop coming for it. We need the numbers on Tuesday."

"We could have Anton experiment on Wednesdays," I teased.

Anton cringed. "We don't want to scare people away. Give me a recipe and I'll make you anything, but ask me to make it up and you're in for trouble."

Everyone laughed. I'd never tasted anything Anton experimented with, so I would have to take his word.

I finished my dinner and went up to my room. I flopped onto my bed and stared at the ceiling. Creepers jumped onto the bed and hopped onto my stomach, then lay on me. He yawned and closed his eyes.

"It's too early for bed," I told him. He ignored me.

I tried to focus on who killed Richard and the mayor. So many people could have done it. I closed my eyes for a minute and felt myself drifting off. If I didn't get up, I was going to be out for the night.

Chapter 16

My eyes popped open when I heard a knock on my door. Creepers was still on my stomach, sound asleep. I heard the door open and someone walking across my living room. It had to be Boyd or Jett. I didn't want to move, and I was sure Creepers didn't.

"Ivy?" Jett said, knocking on my bedroom.

"I can't get up," I said.

The door opened, and he peeked in. "What's wrong?"

"Cat."

He smiled and opened the door. "You let that cat rule over you."

"I don't."

"Then get up."

"He'll wake up."

"Exactly my point."

I smiled. "Can you put my pillow under my head?"

He grabbed it, and I lifted my head so he could shove it under.

"Thanks."

"Another reason I'm a dog person."

"Conan never gets in your bed?"

He looked sheepish. "Maybe occasionally. I don't let him set my sleep schedule, though. I talked to Ned and Ripley."

"What did they say?"

"Ripley said he went to the cave for the locket. He'd gotten it for Mandy and hidden it where Trevor wouldn't find it. Ripley never gave it to her because of all the stuff that happened. He said he went to get it, and someone scared him. According to him, he thought someone was after him. That's why he blocked the entrance."

"Do you believe him?"

"Yeah, but he should have called the police afterward. That's his big problem with everything. He should have turned Trevor in all those years ago."

"What about Ned?"

"He's hiding something. I'm not sure what. I don't know if he's responsible for killing the mayor, but I think he might know who did. We can't hold him for anything, but I told him he can't leave until the investigation is over."

"Who do you think killed Trevor?"

His mouth turned down. "I don't know."

"Did you talk to Kara's parents?"

"Yeah. If they're telling the truth, Spencer's dad would get a little violent. That's why they didn't want Kara going to their property."

"But what was the favor they did for them?"

He sat on the edge of the bed. "Spencer's father hit someone in town. They witnessed it but lied for him. They said they've felt guilty about it ever since."

"Why do they want the farm?"

"Kara's dad said he always wanted it. Combined with his farm, it would be a good investment. They have money saved and want Kara to have the property."

"Do you believe them?"

"Yes. She's their only kid, and they want her to have the best. She's older than me, but I still remember growing up and thinking she had everything."

"My brain is tired. By now, I should at least think I know who's guilty."

He smiled and leaned down, kissing me lightly. "You have to learn to turn it off."

"My brain?"

"Yep. Either that, or stop minding my business for me."

I smiled. "I'm not sure I'm capable of that."

"Someday I won't be sheriff, and then what will you do?"

"Probably get arrested."

"Probably."

Creepers yawned and jumped off my stomach. I sat up. "How do Ledford and Jane interact at work?"

He scratched his jaw. "They don't have to do much together."

"Do they talk?"

"Not a lot."

"Hmm."

"Oh no," he said. "You aren't trying to put Ledford and Jane together, are you? That sounds awful. Did Jane make you mad?"

I laughed. "No, but I still have to find a woman to kiss Ledford."

"You should give up on that. Jane wouldn't fall for him."

"She thinks he's good-looking and tall."

Jett grinned. "Tall? I've never heard him described that way. Of course, Jane is short."

"That means she's at least thought about how he looks."

"He's still got his personality. You would wish that on Jane?"

"What if he just doesn't have any people skills?"

"You already pushed Carrie and José toward each other, and I would almost bet you encouraged Livy toward Anton. Isn't that enough?"

"Ledford might be more pleasant if he were in love."

"I say give it up now. Jane will never fall for Ledford."

"We'll see."

Jett pulled me over so I sat beside him and put his arm over me. "Do you want to make a bet?"

"Such as?"

"You can try your best to get the two of them together. If they go on at least one date before we get married, I'll scoop the litter box for the first year."

"And if they don't?"

"You scoop the litter box and clean up after Conan for a year."

I tapped my lip. Cleaning up after a dog was a lot more effort than cleaning up after a cat. "I win if they go on one date?"

"Yes, but you can't set it up. You can encourage them, but not manipulate it."

"How much time does that give me? We don't even know when we're getting married."

"How long does it take to plan a wedding?"

"Depends."

"On?"

"Who you are and what you want. I want a beautiful dress and a pretty cake. That's all I care about."

He arched his brow. "That's all?"

"What else matters? Even the dress and cake don't really matter in the end. What I really want is you. Spending thousands of dollars and giving myself a bunch of stress seems pointless."

"You don't want to rent out some fancy place?"

"No, but we can if you want to. The church is free."

"I don't care about any of it. I would elope if our moms wouldn't freak out. So when do you want to do it?"

"Well, the elections are coming up. That will keep you busy. Then all the holidays. Then it's cold forever because we live in Kansas."

He frowned. "You want to wait clear until spring?"

I leaned my head against him. "Not really. How about I go find a dress and see how long it takes to be fitted and everything, then we decide?"

"Sounds good."

I stood and smiled. "Now I just have to figure out a way to get Ledford and Jane together."

He groaned. "Poor Jane."

Spencer Cunningham sat at a booth eating a salad. I saw him out the serving window. I wanted to talk to him, but I couldn't think of anything to say.

"Ivy?" Livy said, poking her head in the kitchen door. "Mr. Cunningham wants to talk to you."

Well, that fixed my problem.

I removed my apron and hairnet and went to the dining area.

"You wanted to talk to me?" I asked.

"Yes, can you sit for a minute?"

"Of course." I sat across from him.

He leaned over and said quietly, "I saw my cousin Mandy the other day."

"You did?"

"Yes. I assume that means you found her. I doubt she would come here on her own."

"I did. Did you talk to her?"

"No. She didn't see me. I doubt she would recognize me after forty-five years."

"You recognized her."

"Yeah, she aged well. I assume she dyes her hair. She was with a man. I'm guessing her husband."

"Yes. She said you didn't approve of him."

"Her husband?"

I nodded.

"My parents didn't approve of him. At least if she went off with one of the drifters. They had me try to figure out who he was. My heart wasn't into it."

"Did you know him?"

"No. I just knew he was a drifter."

"Mandy told me you cornered her and told her the man she was in love with was planning to steal from your family."

His eyes narrowed. "She said that? The only time we talked about it was when I told her drifters were usually no-good thieves. She must have taken it more seriously than what I meant. Mandy has an overactive imagination. Too much reading, I believe."

"Are you still trying to buy Barbra's farm?"

"I'm not sure. I heard about the body. That's a bit of a turnoff. I'm kind of surprised the sheriff hasn't been around to talk to me about it. I did live there for a while, and it sounds like the body dates back to that time."

"I'm sure he'll get around to it."

"Who was the dead guy?"

"One of the drifters."

"A friend of Mandy's husband?"

"Yes. The last time anyone saw him, he was delivering a letter to Mandy from his friend."

He sat back. "Who would have killed him?"

I shrugged.

He scratched his head and looked out the window. "There is something I know. I've tried to block it out."

"Oh?"

"One night, right before Mandy left, I heard my dad arguing with someone on the porch. He was yelling. That wasn't odd for my dad, but he seemed extra mad that night. It sounded like it became physical. A few hours later, I saw my dad washing his hands in the kitchen. It looked like he had blood on him. He told me one of the cows cut her leg."

"And you think he was lying?"

He nodded. "I took care of the cows, and I never saw one with any injury. I was scared something bad might have happened, but I was afraid of my father, so I kept quiet. I never heard of anyone disappearing or getting hurt, so I convinced myself it was nothing."

"You think your father killed the drifter?"

"I don't know. It's just a gut feeling. I bet they argued, and my dad grabbed a shovel and hit him with it. He probably didn't mean to kill him. It was that temper of his."

I chewed on the inside of my cheek as I thought.

"I have a confession," he said.

"Another one?"

He nodded. "For all these years, I've suspected my father might have killed someone. He told us to stay away from the trees because he'd sprayed them with something. He made us all promise we wouldn't go near them. That seemed off to me, so I walked around all the trees. One had disturbed dirt. I was almost sure he buried someone there."

"What did you do?"

"When I heard the land was for sale, I panicked. I knew something might be found and tarnish my family's name. I couldn't remember which tree. I only knew it was an elm. I dug around trying to find something."

"So the holes were all you?"

"Yes. I didn't find anything, so I thought I'd been wrong all those years ago. Then I heard about the body."

"You need to tell Jett."

"I was hoping we could avoid that. You're the one who cares about the drifter. Can't you let it go and let the sheriff concentrate on who killed the mayor? I know my dad was no good, but it could hurt my standing in town."

"I guess all you have is speculation," I said. "You don't know for sure your father did it."

"Exactly. So can you let it go?"

I don't let things go. It's not in my personality. "I'll think about it."

He nodded. "Thanks."

I went back to the kitchen and tried to piece this all together. I couldn't keep a clear thought in my head. It was a good time to make cookies.

Chapter 17

"Where have you been?" José asked as I pulled a tray of cookies from the oven.

"What?" I asked. "I've been here."

"Not your mind."

"I've been thinking." I'd spent the entire time I'd mixed the cookies thinking about what Spencer said, and I had one hundred percent decided Jett needed to know.

"Anything interesting?"

"Just about the mayor and the body."

"Do you think you're getting close?"

"I'm not sure." I wasn't going to tell anyone but Jett about Spencer's dad for now. If Spencer's story was true, then the mayor's death was probably unrelated, and it was only a coincidence that the land had been dug up around the same time.

"Have you seen Boyd? He hasn't been around as much lately."

"He's working on his campaign stuff."

"There's no one running against him now."

"No, but Barbra's threatening."

Anton laughed. "I'd vote for Barbra over Boyd."

"I'm not sure," José said. "Barbra might do some weird things."

"So could Boyd. If nothing else, he's sure to get stuck in something."

"True."

"Will someone take the next batch of cookies out of the oven? I need to talk to Jett."

"I can," Anton offered.

"Thanks." I hung up my apron and headed to the sheriff's office.

It wasn't as hot as it had been the last month. It made walking pleasant. When I got to the sheriff's office, Spencer was across the street, sitting on the curb. He waved at me, and I tried not to panic. He had every right to sit on the curb. I waved back. He stood and walked casually toward me.

"Where are you off to?" he asked.

"Sheriff's office."

"Oh? Why?"

"I go there all the time."

"What are you doing this time?"

"Do I need a specific reason?"

"People usually do when they go talk to the law." He stepped toward me, and I moved back.

I forced a small smile. "I'm not usually going for business."

"Oh?"

This guy didn't get a hint. "Jett gets off soon, and we go for a walk before it gets too late."

"Right. The mayor said you two were friends."

I raised my eyebrow.

"Why don't you walk with me?" he asked.

I could think of several reasons. "Jett will be waiting for me." It wasn't true. He usually comes to the diner before we walk.

"I feel like you're going to tell the sheriff about my dad. It could ruin my political ambitions."

"You know Jett and I are getting married, right? We spend a lot of time together."

His eyes narrowed. "I didn't know that. From what the mayor said, I thought it was something else."

"The mayor was—" I couldn't come up with a good word.

"A jerk?"

"Pretty much. I feel bad about what happened to him, but he didn't like me at all."

He nodded. "I understand that. I'll let you go. I hope you'll keep what I told you to yourself."

I swallowed.

"You're going to tell him, aren't you?" He grabbed my arm and started walking, pulling me along.

"Let go," I demanded.

"It's just a friendly walk. You need to listen to me. I want to run for mayor in four years. If word gets out that my dad is a possible murderer, I'll never get voted in."

"Most people can separate people from their parents."

"But some can't."

"You need to let go of my arm."

"Just hear me out."

I reached into my purse and grabbed my pepper spray.

"What's going on?" Ledford asked from behind us. This might have been the first time I was happy to hear Ledford.

Spencer dropped my arm and turned around. "Just out for a walk."

Ledford pointed at my upper arm. "It looks like you were holding on pretty tight there."

I rubbed my arm. He'd had a tight grip.

"We're just talking," Spencer said. "Right, Miss Clark?"

Ledford shook his head. "I know Miss Clark. She was about two seconds away from spraying you with something or kicking you in the face. I've seen that look before."

I smiled and moved closer to Ledford.

Spencer held up his hands. "Hey, I'm not looking for a fight."

"Then I suggest you go."

Spencer hurried away, and I let out a slow breath.

"What was that all about?" he asked.

"Spencer thinks his dad killed Richard Marks, but he doesn't want me to tell anyone. He said it will ruin his political career."

"He thought you would keep a secret from Sheriff Malone?"

"He didn't realize we were together."

"Let's go tell the sheriff."

I nodded.

We went into the office, and Jane greeted me.

"Sheriff Malone just came in ten minutes ago," she told me. "He's on a call and said not to interrupt him."

"I can wait."

"You're going to have a bruise," Ledford said.

I looked at my arm. He was right. I would probably have five. One from each of Spencer's fingers. "It's fine."

"I could tell you were about to do something, so I thought I better get over there."

"I had my hand on my pepper spray."

"I'm confused as to why he told you, of all people. Everyone who lives in this town knows you aren't going to let something go."

"He thinks it's an old enough case so Jett won't put too much effort into it. He figured if I left it alone, nothing would come of it."

"He's wrong there. We would still look into it."

Jett came out of his office. "Ivy, I was just coming to find you. I just got a call from Wichita. There was blood on Richard Marks that didn't belong to him."

My eyes went wide. "Did it belong to Spencer Cunningham's father?"

"No. It belonged to Ripley Higgins."

I covered my mouth. "That's unexpected."

"Why did you think it was Mr. Cunningham?"

I told him everything Spencer told me.

"I need to talk to him," Jett said.

"And now Ivy and I are even," Ledford said.

I cocked my head. "Even for what?"

"You saved me, and I saved you."

"Saved her?" Jett asked.

I rubbed my arm. "Spencer didn't want me to talk to you, so he was trying to pull me away from the office and talk me out of telling you."

"He did that?" Jett touched my arm lightly.

"I don't think he was trying to hurt me. He was just trying to get me to walk away from the office."

Jett made a fist. "That doesn't make it all right. I'm going to talk to him now."

"Don't go when you're angry," Ledford said. "That's never a good idea. Sleep on it and go tomorrow."

Jett clenched his teeth. "I'll still be angry tomorrow."

"Then let me go."

"No, I'm going to get to the bottom of this."

I took his arm. "Don't go yet. Make sure you're calm. Tell me more about Ripley."

He took a deep breath. "His blood was on Richard's shirt."

"So Spencer might have been wrong. Ripley might have done it."

"It's hard to say. They've determined the cause of death was blunt trauma to the head. Probably a shovel."

"Did he have anything with him besides the watch?"

"Five dollars and a mint."

"That's not a lot to go by."

"Nope. I'm going to call Ripley and see if he'll come back to talk to me. If not, I'll have to send someone from Topeka. He's been cooperative so far, so I'm hoping he'll come."

"I hope Mandy isn't involved," I said, "but now I wonder. Especially since you said she wouldn't have known her uncle died."

"She could have searched online out of curiosity."

"I suppose so. What about the mayor? Did Ripley come back and do that?"

Ledford shook his head. "I bet it's separate. Ned seems awfully guilty to me."

"He does," Jett agreed. "Getting proof is hard. No cameras in the neighborhood picked up anyone walking around nearby. Ned admits he was there, but not to tampering with anything."

"Is Boyd cleared of everything?" I asked.

"Yes. I'm not sure whether someone tried to plant his debit card or if he dropped it, but either way, we know he was at the site talking to people."

"Did you check the card for prints?"

"Yes. There were only his and yours."

"Do you still want to go for a walk?"

He nodded. "But I'm still going to talk to Spencer in the morning, and I can't promise I'll be calm."

"Hey, Ledford called me Ivy a minute ago. Does that mean we're friends?"

Ledford crossed his arms. "I don't think I did."

Jett smiled slightly. "I heard it."

"Does that mean I can start calling you..." I had no idea what Ledford's first name was. "Bob?"

He snorted. "My name isn't Bob."

"Harold? Bart?"

His mouth twitched in the corner.

"Kaz," Jett said. "Kaz Rupert Ledford."

"Thanks a lot," Ledford muttered.

I smiled. "Your name is Kaz? I never would have come up with that."

"And I don't want it getting around."

"It's not that bad," Jett said with a smirk.

"You can call me Deputy Ledford. If we ever do become friends, you can call me Ledford."

Chapter 18

Something was going on in the diner, but I wasn't sure what. It sounded like arguing. I was almost finished curling my hair, then I would go down. If it was anything too bad, José would deal with it.

The voices were louder now, so I hurried down to the diner. Ripley and Spencer stood in the middle of the dining area, glaring at each other. José tried to get them to quiet down, but they ignored him. Mandy sat at a booth, her face pale.

"What's going on?" I asked.

"Jett's on his way," José said.

Boyd sat at a booth eating a stack of pancakes, and in the booth behind him was Ned. How did all of these people end up here at the same time? There was no one else in the diner except the staff.

The door opened, and Jett entered. "What's the problem?" he asked.

"He's trying to accuse me of murder!" Spencer said, pointing at Ripley. "I've never spoken to this man in my life, and he's trying to point his finger at me."

"I'd almost bet you killed Trevor."

"Who is Trevor? I never killed anyone."

"Richard Marks. He was my traveling companion."

"Why would you think I killed him? This is ridiculous."

Jett pointed at a booth behind Ned. "Go sit, Spencer. I'll talk to you after I talk to Ripley."

Spencer slunk over to the booth. He knocked Ned's jacket from the booth, picked it up, and tossed it back onto the bench, then sank down onto the bench behind him.

"Ripley, talk," Jett said.

"The day I left Muddy Creek, I fought with Trevor. He told me he was leaving without me. He called me a bunch of names, and we had a little fistfight."

"Did you bleed?" Jett asked.

"Yeah. He started it all by punching me. He gave me a bloody lip. I jumped on him, and we rolled around in the dirt. He grabbed the letter he'd agreed to deliver to Mandy. He yelled that he would deliver my stupid letter, and then he was done. I told him not to bother, but he stomped away. That was the last time I ever saw him."

"What did you do after that?" I asked.

"I sat and waited, hoping Mandy would come. A while later, she did. She had tears running down her cheeks. I explained to her that her cousin had lied to her. I was never going to steal anything. She believed me. She told me she would leave with me, but we had to leave right then. I asked why. She said she saw something and didn't want to talk about it. That it was too terrible."

"What did she see?"

"She never told me. I brought up Spencer a few times, and she would get upset and tell me never to mention his name. I figure she saw him kill Trevor. She still won't tell me."

"You are accusing me of something you have no proof of!" Spencer growled.

"No proof, but I'm right."

Jett turned to Mandy. She was covering her face with her hands. "Mandy?"

"I'm not talking about it," she said.

"Ripley's blood was found on the body."

She looked up and frowned.

"That's because he punched me in the face."

Spencer sneered. "It looks like you're accusing me because you're guilty."

"I did see it," Mandy said at almost a whisper. "Spencer was arguing with someone out front. When I peeked out the window, I saw him hit the man with something. I didn't know Trevor, so I wasn't sure what was happening.

Spencer dragged him behind the house. I suspected he was Ripley's friend, so I ran to the tree and found the letter he wrote. I ran immediately to Ripley, and we left."

"That's a lie," Spencer said.

I stared at him. "You told me your father probably hit Trevor with a shovel or something. No one even knew that was the way he died until last night."

"I didn't know what happened. I was guessing."

I walked over to Ned. "Can I see your jacket?"

Ned frowned, but handed it to me. I searched the pockets. I felt something hard and small. Pulling it out, I opened my hand. Two long screws lay there.

"What are those?" Ned asked. "I didn't put them there."

"My guess is they are some of the screws that were taken out of the scaffolding that caused the mayor's death."

"I swear I didn't do it."

"No. Spencer put them there when he knocked your coat off the bench."

"Why would I do that?" Spencer asked.

"To make Ned look more guilty than he already did."

Boyd swallowed his pancake and pointed to the corner of the diner. "There are cameras right there. It won't be hard to watch and see you put the screws there."

The blood drained from Spencer's face.

He turned and glared at me.

"Don't even look at her," Jett said. "You're lucky I haven't punched you for bruising her arm yesterday."

Spencer charged toward Jett, but I slammed into him before he could reach him, knocking us both to the floor. Jett pulled me to my feet to get me out of the way, and Boyd smashed his plate over Spencer's head. He looked dazed for a moment.

Jett grabbed Spencer and handcuffed him. Ned tried to sneak out of the diner, but José blocked the door.

"Talk, Ned."

Ned sighed. "The mayor gave me five thousand dollars to pay off Macey. I got an anonymous call the same day telling me that if I took Mayor Jepson to the condo site on a certain day and had him stand on the scaffolding, they would pay me two thousand dollars. I asked why. They said they wanted to take a picture of him staring out at the city from up there, like he thought he was some sort of king or something."

"And you agreed?" Jett asked.

"I knew the mayor was going to fire me. I was happy to let him look bad. I agreed, and the next day, there was an envelope in my mailbox with two thousand dollars in it. There was a note that said if I didn't deliver, I would regret it. I believed it. When the date came, I'd already convinced the mayor he needed to go to the site."

"And he just listened when you told him to go stand in that certain spot?" I asked.

"I told him someone was coming to take a picture of him to make him look good. He didn't hesitate. I thought a photographer was hidden somewhere. He climbed up and fell. I panicked and ran."

"You didn't think it might be an accident and stay to call for help?" Jett asked.

"No. The first thing I thought was that someone was trying to frame me."

"This is all ridiculous," Spencer muttered.

"The camera will prove it," I said.

"Why would you kill the drifter?" Mandy asked her cousin. "What did he do to you?"

Spencer glared at her. "This is all your fault. If you had listened to my parents, none of this would have happened. You should have stayed away from that man."

"I'd never met him!"

"I mean that one," he said, pointing at Ripley.

"Who's been taking all the money Trevor stole from the bank?" Boyd asked.

"My guess is Spencer," Jett said. "He probably saw the watch with the location, wrote it down, then buried it."

"That's not true. I don't know anything about a cave."

Jett smiled. "No one said anything about a cave."

Spencer's face burned red.

"The cash in the envelope was old," Ned said. "I thought it was odd."

Jett nodded. "The bank where Ned deposited the money matched the money from a bank robbery forty-five years ago. The bank was suspicious and opened an investigation."

"That drifter came to my house and disrespected me!" Spencer yelled. "I told him to get off my land, and he told me he goes where he wants. I thought he was the one who was bothering my cousin. Things got heated. I didn't mean to kill him. As for the mayor, he shouldn't have been trying to change things that no one wants changed except him!"

The room was quiet for a moment.

"Well, that sure sounds like a confession to me," Boyd said.

Jett pulled Spencer to his feet. "I need everyone to stay at the diner until I've had time to talk to you." He led Spencer from the diner.

"How did all these people end up here?" I asked.

"We ran into Spencer when we came in," Ripley said.

"Ned was walking by, and I told him to come in," José said. "I figured we might as well get it all figured out with everyone at once. We lost a few customers when the fighting began."

Ripley frowned and looked at me. "Sorry about that. I'm also sorry for the cave. You scared me to death when I touched your arm. I wasn't thinking straight until I was halfway back to town. I drove back to unblock the cave entrance, but someone was already there."

"It's alright," I said. "I'm just glad it all worked out."

"I've tried to block all of this out for years," Mandy said. "I bet I'm going to be questioned a lot before it's over."

Ripley put his arm around her. "I'm sorry you've been living with this all these years. I wish you would have told me. I always knew something bothered you."

"I've felt guilty all this time for not telling anyone what I saw."

"Now we can deal with it."

She nodded, and they hugged.

"The people at the bank commented on the money," Ned said. "I was worried they wouldn't take it. They did, but they were giving me strange looks. I'm just glad it's all over."

Everyone murmured in agreement. I wondered how over it was. All of them could end up in trouble for things they'd done. Not as much as Spencer would be, though. I just hoped Mandy could get past it and live the rest of her life in peace.

Chapter 19

"Oh, good. You're still here," I said when I entered the library.

Brian looked up from his computer. "Hi, Ivy. I'm usually here."

"I thought you were leaving to help those people start a library."

He nodded. "Not yet. I want to make sure the people I've hired here have everything under control."

"How many people will work here?"

"Three."

I leaned against the desk. "Wow. How did you hire people so fast? I've been trying to get more people to work at the diner, and I can't even get people to apply."

He smiled. "The diner might need to offer hazard pay. I heard about everything that went down there yesterday."

"Yes. Thanks for all your help. I never would have figured it out without you."

He nodded. "That's what I'm here for."

Brian's cat Paisley walked lazily over to the desk. He bent down and picked her up.

"Who's going to watch your cats while you're gone?"

"I'll drive back and forth so they shouldn't have too much trouble. My brother's going to be staying in town for a while. He's doing some online college courses, so he wants to be in a place with fewer distractions than the city. He can keep an eye out to make sure they're all okay. Most of them are outdoor cats, anyway."

"It'll be rough not to be able to pop in every time I have a question."

"You can call me anytime."

"Thanks, Brian. You've always been a great friend."

His mouth turned down, but then formed a smile. "Always glad to help."

I wondered if Brian really did like me. He was acting a little different since he found out Jett and I were getting married. I couldn't imagine Jett was really right. The entire town new Jett and I were likely to end up together almost from the beginning. Brian knew we were dating, and he'd never acted strange.

"Is everything alright?" I couldn't help asking. "You've seemed a little different lately."

Brian shrugged. "I've been doing the same thing for so long. I'm excited to make a change, but it's still stressful."

"That makes sense. Let me know if you need anything." Jett had been wrong. He was just distracted by getting the library ready and going to his new job.

"Thanks. Oh, and I got this for Creepers." He put Paisley down, reached under his desk, and pulled out a cat toy.

"You don't have to buy things for Creepers. You spoil him."

He smiled a genuine smile. "Since Paisley is his mom, I feel like I'm his grandpa or something."

"Well, thank you. He appreciates it. And you aren't old enough to be a grandpa."

He laughed. "I am in cat years. I'm going to be forty-six this year. That's probably old enough to be a grandpa in people years, too."

"I'd better get going. Boyd wants to talk to me about his campaign."

"Tell him good luck. He can put a sign in the library if he wants."

"I will."

I walked over to Jett and Boyd's place with Brian on my mind. I hoped the new job would make him happy.

Boyd was sitting outside on the porch with Conan. The dog ran over when he saw me. I scooped him up and rubbed his head.

"Hey, buddy," I said, sitting on the step by Boyd.

"He likes you. Even though you're a cat person."

"You're a cat person."

He chuckled. "Yeah, but I'm a cat and dog person. I don't show favoritism."

"Conan's the size of a cat."

"And I've taught him to use a litter box."

"Nice." It would be really nice if I lost my bet with Jett and had to clean up after him for a year.

"Should I be running for mayor?" he asked. "I've been thinking about it. I didn't get to help you as much as I would like to when you're solving a case, just because I'm running."

"But as mayor, you can make good changes. Jett said being mayor of Muddy Creek is less than a part-time job. Just a few hours a week."

"I guess that's right."

"Have you known Brian his whole life?"

"Yep."

"Has he ever been in a relationship?"

"Uh-oh. Are you trying to set Brian up with someone?"

"No. I'm just curious. I feel like Brian's a good friend, but I don't know anything about his social life."

Boyd nodded. "Brian is a good guy. He's friendly, but at the same time, he still keeps to himself. I've never known him to have a girlfriend, but I could be wrong."

"He told me once that he should have gotten married when he was younger. He said he has bad taste."

"Then you must know more than I do. I'm just happy you stopped trying to set me up with Barbra. I'd rather you try to pair Brian up with someone."

"You like Barbra."

"Maybe. We're too different."

"Well, you don't have to worry. Ledford's my next target."

Boyd blinked twice. "Ledford? You think you can find a woman anywhere on this planet to fall for Ledford?"

I laughed. "He's not as bad as he used to be."

"I'm going to enjoy watching this."

"As the mayor?"

He sighed. "I suppose."

"You don't have to do it."

"I should. I need something to do, and if I don't, who will? Brian should have run. He would have made a good mayor."

I nodded. "But you will be too."

"I hope so."

Conan jumped off my lap to chase a butterfly.

"Now that the case is solved, what will you do? There isn't anything fun happening until the holidays roll around."

I shrugged. "I guess I'll be bored. Or plan my wedding."

"Right, right. I almost forgot about that. It's about time. You two sure dragged your feet long enough."

I grinned. "We haven't even been dating for a year."

"It feels longer. Probably because everyone knew you should be dating before you started."

I smiled when I thought about the first time I'd seen Jett. I had definitely been interested right away. I'd been in Muddy Creek for over a year now, and it did feel like it had been longer.

"I'm going to the diner. Do you want to come?"

"Yes. I haven't had a cookie in two days."

I stood and smiled. "That's pretty sad."

Chapter 20

"Everyone, sit!" José commanded the people gathered in the party room. I was already sitting at a table next to Jett. On the other side of him were his parents. The chattering all died down as people found seats. Almost every chair was full.

José stood at the front of the room. "Thanks to all of you who have attended to celebrate the election results. If you haven't heard, Boyd Webster is now Mayor Webster." He paused while people clapped and called out. "And Sheriff Malone has been elected for another four years." More cheering.

Jett leaned toward me. "It would be more impressive if either one of us had been running against someone."

I kissed his cheek. "You still would have won."

"Mayor Webster, do you want to say anything?" José asked.

Boyd stood. "Well, thanks for voting for me. I know it was a close race." Everyone laughed. "I'll do my best for Muddy Creek. If I'm failing, I hope my friends here will let me know and help me succeed. Thank you."

Everyone clapped.

"Sheriff?" José asked.

Jett got up. "I know what everyone's thinking. Why didn't Ivy run?" Everyone smiled. "I'm sure she would have if she qualified, and she would have won."

I rolled my eyes.

"I'm here for all of you, whatever you need. Muddy Creek has a lot of good people, and I'm grateful for all the support you have shown the department and me. We're all going to make Muddy Creek a coveted place to live."

"I hope so, or there are going to be a lot of empty condos!" someone teased.

Jett smiled. "From what I hear, the condos are selling well. They could raise the town population by one-tenth. That could put some strain on the city, but the mayor and I will work together in hopes of making a smooth transition."

"Will Barbra's land be developed?" someone asked.

"Not at this time," Boyd said. "It's been purchased by Kara Wilson."

Jett sat back down, and Boyd answered more questions about development. I was almost positive he made up half the answers as he went.

Livy and the other servers brought in trays of food and put them in front of everyone. José's enchiladas were always a hit, so that was what we decided to serve. This was all happening after hours so the people who worked here could join. The servers took their seats as soon as the food was passed around.

"Can I say something?" Ledford stood. Everyone stopped talking and turned to watch him. "When I was working with Miss Clark on this last case, I had an idea. A geocaching competition."

"A what now?" Barbra asked.

"Geocaching. People all over make containers and hide them. You download an app on your phone that gives you an approximate location and a clue. When you find the container, you open it. Some have items inside. You can take them out and exchange them for something. Some are so small that all they have is a rolled-up paper. You write your name on the paper and put it back in its hiding place."

"What's the point?" Opal asked.

"Well, it's fun. It's like a treasure hunt."

"With no treasure?"

"It depends on your point of view."

"And people hide them all over?" Barbra asked.

"Yes. It's a big thing."

"Then why haven't we heard of it?"

Anton grinned. "Because you're—"

"Old?"

"I was going to say seasoned."

Barbra laughed. "I am seasoned. I doubt there are many of those things in Muddy Creek."

"There are actually several." Ledford pulled out his phone and showed us the screen. This is a close-up of Muddy Creek. All these smiley faces are the ones I've found."

There were quite a few.

"For our competition, we would split into teams and see who finds the most in a month."

"But you've already found all of those," Anton said. "I've found ten this year and most people don't have any."

"I'll be in charge, so I won't compete."

"Who makes them?" I asked. "Especially around here?"

Ledford shrugged. "Most of them have been hidden by the same person, but they have a nickname."

"And people actually find them?"

"Yes. When people pass through town, they look. I see people off in the bushes all the time."

I'd seen that as well, but I always figured they lost something.

"You're supposed to try to do it unseen."

"When will this happen?" Jett asked.

"December?"

I wrinkled my nose. "In the snow?"

He smiled. It was always weird to see Ledford smile. "That adds to the challenge. I'll work for the next few months on adding some more. I've put about twenty around town since I've been here. So who's in?"

Everyone looked around. It sounded cold to me. In the spring, I would be all for it. Still, this was the first time Ledford had reached out to the town.

"I'm in," I said. "How many on a team?"

"No more than five."

"I'm with Ivy," Jett said.

"Me too," Boyd said, holding up a hand.

By the time the evening was over, Ledford had a list of four teams. I was sure the list would grow once the rest of the town heard about it. I would work on convincing Ledford to wait until spring. It was after midnight once we had everything clean.

Jett put the mop into the cleaning closet and yawned. "You really want to go digging through the snow to solve riddles?"

"I'm not excited about the snow, but the rest sounds fun."

"We're taking off," José said, grabbing Carrie's hand. "See you tomorrow."

I flipped off all the kitchen lights and went to check the dining area one last time. Jett came behind me.

He tossed something in the trash. "It was nice of you to volunteer. I don't think anyone would have if you hadn't."

"Ledford's putting forth an effort. I didn't know he ever did anything fun. I wanted to be encouraging."

"If it keeps you occupied and not in danger, then it's got my vote."

"What will you do once your next term is over?"

"What do you mean?"

"You can only get elected as sheriff twice, right?"

"Not in Kansas. So long as you win, you can go on forever."

"Oh. So you'll run again in four years?"

"I dunno. I might. We'll have to see when it gets closer."

"What's going to happen to Mandy?"

"I'm not sure. Everyone involved will have to go to court."

"Do you think she'll go to jail for not telling on Spencer?"

"I doubt it, but I can't say. The judge will decide. Ripley could go to jail for not telling anyone Trevor was stealing things, and Ned could go for taking a bribe that caused a death. I don't think Ripley and Mandy will get into too much trouble. Ned, I'm not so sure about."

"I should start keeping a journal. I haven't been bored a lot since I moved here."

He wrapped his arms around me and kissed me softly. "Nothing with you is ever boring."

Chocolate Almond Biscotti

Ingredients:

10 tbsp (141 g) unsalted butter, softened

1⅓ cups (265 g) sugar

3 large eggs

2 tsp vanilla extract *(or 1–2 tsp anise extract, if desired)*

3¼ cups (406 g) all-purpose flour

1 tbsp baking powder

¾ tsp salt

⅔ cup (66 g) slivered almonds

⅔ cup (113 g) mini chocolate chips

½ cup (170 g) dark chocolate wafers or chips (optional, for dipping)

Instructions:

Preheat oven to 350°F (175°C). Line a baking sheet with parchment.

Beat butter and sugar until creamy. Add eggs one at a time, mixing well. Stir in vanilla.

In another bowl, whisk flour, baking powder, and salt. Gradually add to wet mixture.

Stir in almonds and chocolate chips.

Divide dough in half. On a floured surface, shape into two 10–12" x 2–3" logs. Place on baking sheet, 4" apart.

Bake 30 minutes, until golden. Cool completely. *(Leave oven on or set a reminder.)*
Slice diagonally into 1½" pieces. Place cut-side down on sheet.
Bake 10 minutes, flip, then bake another 10 minutes.
Cool completely. Drizzle with melted chocolate if desired.

Notes:
Swap or omit add-ins as preferred.
Store in airtight container for 2 weeks or freeze for several months.

Special thanks to Sam at https://sugarspunrun.com for sharing her recipe.

Also By Kristy Dixon

<u>Cozy Mystery</u>
Murder With a Side of Bacon
Murder With a Hint of Cinnamon
Murder With a Fudge Brownie to Go
Murder With a Splash of Vanilla
Murder With a Drizzle of Syrup
Murder With a Slice of Pie
Murder With a Swirl of Blueberry
Suite Lies and Alibis
Not So Suite Caroline

<u>Young Adult</u>
The Silver Eclipse (3 books)
The Amethyst Crown
More Than Once Upon a Time
Trapped In Once Upon a Time
The Beginning of Once Upon a Time
Riviand Lost (4 books)

<u>Coming Soon!</u>
Murder With a Sip of Eggnog
Forgotten in Once Upon a Time
Rise of the Serpent (Riviand Lost Book 5)

About the Author

Kristy Dixon started writing stories at age seven and never stopped. These days, she writes cozy mysteries full of quirky characters, small-town charm, and the occasional dead body. She also writes YA novels when the teens in her head get too loud to ignore. Kristy lives with her husband, kids, one spoiled cat, and a flock of chickens who think they run the place. When she's not writing or wrangling her crew, she's likely playing board games, plotting murders (fictional, of course), or dreaming about cookies.

www.ingramcontent.com/pod-product-compliance
Lightning Source LLC
Chambersburg PA
CBHW031530310726
48971CB00008B/2427